TORI LOSES CONTROL

She was skating beautifully and it felt wonderful.
Maybe it was because she was relaxed. Maybe
that was the secret, Tori thought. She just needed
to do more yoga and do Dan's breathing exercises. And forget about how well everyone else
was skating, and whether she'd bomb at Nationals.

Tori began to slow the spin. As she did, she
knew right away that something was wrong. The
ice beneath her skates was shifting, tilting one
way and then another, even after she'd come to a
complete stop.

In a panic, she reached out for something to
hold on to. But her fingers gripped only the empty
air. Her stomach lurched as the white ice suddenly rose up to meet her.

A second later, everything went black.

Other Skylark Books you will enjoy
Ask your bookseller for the books you have missed

Gold Medal Dreams #1
ON THE EDGE

Melissa Lowell

Created by Parachute Press, Inc.

A SKYLARK BOOK
NEW YORK • TORONTO • LONDON • SYDNEY • AUCKLAND

With special thanks to Darlene Parent, director of
Sky Rink Skating School, New York City,
and the choreographer of Tori's skating routines

RL 5.2, 009–012
ON THE EDGE
A Skylark Book / December 1997

Skylark Books is a registered trademark of Bantam Books,
a division of Bantam Doubleday Dell Publishing Group, Inc.
Registered in U.S. Patent and Trademark Office and elsewhere.

Silver Blades® is a registered trademark of Parachute Press, Inc.
The logos of the United States Figure Skating Association
("USFSA") are the property of USFSA and used herein by
permission of USFSA. All other rights reserved by USFSA. USFSA
assumes no responsibility for the contents of this book.

ISBN 0-553-48515-6

Published simultaneously in the United States and Canada

Bantam Books are published by Bantam Books, a division of
Bantam Doubleday Dell Publishing Group, Inc. Its trademark,
consisting of the words "Bantam Books" and the portrayal of a
rooster, is Registered in the U.S. Patent and Trademark Office and in
other countries. Marca Registrada. Bantam Books, 1540 Broadway,
New York, New York 10036.

PRINTED IN THE UNITED STATES OF AMERICA

OPM   0   9   8   7   6   5   4   3   2   1

1

*B*ANG!

Tori Carsen sat up with a start.

"Four more weeks, Tori," a voice called.

Tori shook her head. For a second she didn't know where she was. Then she felt the hard bench she was sitting on. She was in the girls' locker room at the Seneca Hills Ice Arena. Her good friend Martina Nemo had just burst through the door.

Tori couldn't believe it. She'd fallen asleep sitting in the warm, steamy room before morning skating practice. How embarrassing. She hoped Martina hadn't noticed. She took a quick, deep breath and sat up straight. What had Martina said? Four more weeks?

"Oh, until Nationals, you mean." Tori swallowed a yawn.

"Earth to Tori," Martina joked. "Of course I mean

Nationals! Did you forget that little detail? The one about how you're skating in the country's most important amateur competition? It's in four weeks, by the way, in case you want to start getting ready."

Tori grinned. "It's not four weeks, Martina. It's three weeks, six days, seven hours, and"—Tori checked her watch—"eighteen minutes."

"Yeah, but who's counting?" Martina laughed.

Martina pulled off her parka and plopped down on the narrow wooden bench. Her shiny dark brown hair swung over one cheek as she leaned down to pull her skates from her bag.

"Nationals are such a big deal," Martina went on. "You must be scared stiff."

"Who, me?" Tori said, brushing her long blond ponytail off her shoulder. "Nah. I'm not nervous. See?" She held out a hand and made her fingers tremble wildly. Then she grabbed it with her other hand and yanked it into her lap. The girls giggled.

"Well, I'm sure you'll do great, Tori," Martina said. "If anyone can deal with the pressure of Nationals, you can. You're the most confident skater in Silver Blades."

Silver Blades was one of the best skating clubs in the country. Twice a year, dozens of kids from the United States and other countries traveled to Seneca Hills, Pennsylvania, to try out. Of those, only a few were accepted into Silver Blades.

"Of course I'm the most confident member," Tori told Martina. "And I'm the most modest, too!"

Martina smiled and shook her head. "You're so silly!"

Tori was making jokes because she didn't want to tell Martina that she *was* nervous about Nationals. No, not nervous—*scared stiff,* to use Martina's words.

Tori had joined Silver Blades when she was only eight years old. Competing at Nationals and then the Olympics had been her dream ever since.

Now her dream was becoming real. It was the scariest—and the most exciting—feeling Tori had ever had! She would be competing against the very best skaters in the country at Nationals, which would be held in nearby Philadelphia this year. Only the top three finishers would go on to the Olympics. Tori needed all the confidence she could get. She hoped that if she *acted* confident, she might really become confident!

Tori snapped back to attention as Martina continued chatting. "Your mom must be psyched," Martina remarked.

Tori nodded. Her mother was known at the rink for pushing Tori very hard. She rarely missed a practice, and she sometimes yelled at Tori from the boards if Tori didn't skate well. Corinne Carsen had been an accomplished skater herself once, but she had never made it to Nationals. Now she hoped Tori would live out her dream.

"Mom is excited," Tori admitted. "But, believe it or not, she's calmed down about my skating since she married Roger a few months ago. She only comes to about *half* my practices now."

Roger Arnold was Tori's stepfather. Her real father, James Carsen, had moved out shortly after she was born. They had seen each other only once since then.

It used to hurt Tori's feelings that her father didn't call or write. But now that she was fifteen, she had written off her father as someone she couldn't count on.

"Well, it must be a relief that your mother has other stuff to pay attention to besides your skating," Martina said. She slipped rubber guards onto the blades of her skates, then stood up and walked to her locker.

"See you on the ice in a few, Tor," Martina called. She slammed the locker shut and headed to the rink.

"Okay," Tori replied. "See you out there."

Tori slipped on her skate guards and started for the door. As she passed a full-length mirror, she paused. She touched the rhinestones around the neck of her violet skating dress. They sparkled and caught the light.

Tori's outfits were always dressier than the leggings and sweatshirts the other girls wore to practice. Tori's mother was a fashion designer. That was how she'd met Roger. Her boutique, Carsen Design Group, was in the big department store Roger owned, called Arnold's. Mrs. Carsen had kept her last name after the wedding. She wanted her customers to know she was still the Carsen in Carsen Design Group.

Mrs. Carsen made all Tori's skating outfits. She always told Tori that if she dressed like a champion, she'd skate like one too.

The problem was, these days Tori didn't *feel* like a champion. She was always tired. She didn't understand how that could be possible. If she wasn't skating or at school, she was sleeping. And now she was even dozing off in public. So why didn't she feel rested?

Tori thought half the reason she was tired was because she had competed at the Eastern Division Sectionals in Connecticut a couple of weeks ago. Her body still hadn't . . . *bounced back* the way it always did after she gave her all at a big competition.

And Tori had only placed third at Sectionals. That was barely enough to qualify her for Nationals. Her coach, Dan Trapp, said she needed to change her routine if she was going to medal at the U.S. Figure Skating Championships, otherwise known as Nationals.

Tori's new routine was hard. The hardest she had ever skated. Trying to perfect it was the other reason she was exhausted, she thought.

Dan had pulled her aside after practice one afternoon, shortly after Sectionals, to describe the new routine.

"It will have *two* triple-triple jump combinations!" he said, his eyes shining. "No female figure skater has ever done that in competition. But *you* can, Tori. I know it."

Tori walked into the rink area and did some stretches. Then she took off her skate guards and stepped onto the ice. She skated around a few times to warm up her muscles.

She started practicing her routine, moving into

back crossovers to pick up speed for a double axel. Then she curved into a serpentine pattern of steps. She landed a triple Lutz perfectly.

Cool air rushed over her face as she circled the rink. She thought ahead to the first triple-triple jump combination.

Tori soared into an inside spiral, then alternating Mohawks. Her steps were light and playful. She moved into powerful back crossovers. She gained speed and leaped into the triple toe loop–triple toe loop.

The jumps were high and tight, and she landed solidly.

Yes! she thought, taking a deep breath.

She pushed on with her new routine, doing a tricky combination spin. She moved through the graceful footwork that led up to a triple salchow jump. Then she did a layback spin, arching her back and straining to keep her position.

Tori was breathing hard by now. She did a beautiful spiral sequence, holding her leg high and still. Then she set up for her second triple-triple combination jump, a triple loop–triple loop. It was the hardest part of her routine because she was always tired by then.

But today Tori soared into the jumps. She felt as if she were flying! She landed easily and a huge grin spread across her face. She did more footwork, then sped into a split jump and a stag leap. She ended the routine with a dramatic death drop.

Tori held the ending for a few seconds. Then she stood up straight and punched her fist in the air.

"Yes!" she cried.

She sighed happily and skated over to the boards. Her soft purple skirt swung as she stopped crisply and picked up a towel. She blotted sweat off her forehead and glanced around the ice. It was only six-thirty in the morning, but the rink was getting crowded and noisy as other members of Silver Blades arrived.

Tori dropped the towel back on the rail and turned around. Just then, Patrick McGuire zipped past her. Tori's best friend, Haley Arthur, was right behind him.

"Hey, watch it, you guys," Tori called out. "You almost flattened me!"

"Sorry, Tori," Patrick yelled over his shoulder.

"Me too," Haley shouted. A second later, she caught up with Patrick and tagged him on the shoulder. "You're it, Patrick!" she cried.

Tori laughed as Haley zoomed off. No way would Patrick catch up with her. The two had been skating pairs together in Silver Blades for almost a year. Haley knew all Patrick's moves. She dodged, then glided away, screaming.

Patrick suddenly spun around. He made a beeline for Tori.

"Gotcha!" he said, tagging her on the shoulder and racing off.

Tori hesitated. With Nationals so close, she was supposed to spend every free minute working on her new routine. She didn't have time to play tag.

Suddenly Haley was twirling in front of her. Her best friend always knew how to make Tori react.

"Nah, nah," Haley said, sticking her thumbs in her ears and wiggling her fingers. "You can't get me!" Her green eyes glimmered with mischief. She skated backward, just a few feet away, taunting Tori.

Tori giggled. "Oh yes I can!" she cried. As Haley took off across the rink, Tori darted after her.

Haley had a good head start, but Tori was fast. She bent her knees deeply to increase her speed. Soon she was practically flying over the ice.

"There's no escape, Haley," Tori yelled as the gap between them narrowed. "Now I'm going to get—"

Just as Tori reached out to tag Haley, her left leg buckled. It felt as if her muscles had suddenly stopped working.

Then Tori's leg gave way completely. For a second, she flailed her arms, struggling to keep her balance. She felt as if everything were moving in slow motion.

Tori crashed onto the ice—*hard*. She grunted as she landed on her stomach and skidded across the ice. Laughter rang out from the other side of the rink.

"Whoa! Nice fall, Tori," Patrick hooted. "I'd give it a five-nine score!"

Haley laughed too. "I told you you couldn't catch me," she called over her shoulder, her auburn hair bouncing.

Tori didn't answer them. She just lay there, sprawled on the ice.

What just happened? she wondered. She couldn't

figure out why she had fallen. She hadn't lost her balance. She hadn't felt her foot hit a chink in the ice. She gazed at the surface of the rink. She couldn't spot any nicks or scratches in the fresh ice. She had fallen a million times, but she always knew the reason. This felt different.

Haley skated over. As she came closer, her grin turned into a frown.

"Hey," she said, "are you okay, Tori?" Haley held out a hand.

"Yeah, I'm fine," Tori said. She took Haley's hand and quickly stood. "Thanks," she said.

"No problem," Haley answered. "Nice move," she added with a grin. "Make sure you show it to the judges at Nationals."

Tori groaned. "Don't worry," she said. "There's no way I'm going to fall like that at Nationals. My program is going to be perfect."

2

"Tori, wake up! It's morning."

Tori stirred. She tried to open her eyes, but it felt as if lead weights lay on her lids. It was the second time in two days someone had forced her awake.

"Come on," Natalia Cherkas said. She shook Tori's shoulder. "Get up. You can't sleep all day."

"Why not?" Tori groaned. She rolled onto her back and opened her eyes. "It's Sunday. We don't have to go to the rink today."

Natalia nudged Tori again. Natalia was a pretty, dark-haired Russian girl. Her mother had died when she was very young. The fourteen-year-old had moved to the United States with her father a few months ago. He was a busy diplomat in Washington, D.C. So busy, he had arranged for Natalia to live with the Carsens.

That way, she had a family life, and she could train with Silver Blades.

"Tori, you promised that we would go to the mall today," Natalia reminded her. "I want to buy jeans. Get up!"

"I thought we weren't going until eleven," Tori said sleepily. She sat up and yawned. "What time is it, anyway?"

"It's almost ten o'clock!" Natalia told her.

"Ten o'clock?" Tori repeated. She couldn't believe it. She always got up at the crack of dawn for practice. It was such a habit, she automatically woke up early on Sundays, too.

When was the last time I slept this late? she wondered.

"That's right," Natalia said happily. "It's almost ten. The mall will be open in an hour."

Tori climbed out of bed and started getting dressed. She grinned at Natalia's eager expression. A few months ago, Natalia had been so homesick, she'd wanted to return to Russia. Now she loved Pennsylvania. And she especially loved Canady's—her favorite clothing store in the Seneca Hills Mall!

A few minutes later, Tori and Natalia walked into the kitchen. Tori's mother looked up from her newspaper and smiled at the girls.

"So what's the plan for today, you two?" Mrs. Carsen asked. "Still going shopping at the mall?"

Tori nodded. "Yup. And then we're meeting Haley and everybody else at Super Sundaes." She poured herself a bowl of whole-grain cereal and carried it to the table. "Can you give us a ride, Mom?" she asked, sitting down.

Mrs. Carsen didn't reply. Instead, she stared intently at Tori across the table.

"What?" Tori said uncomfortably. She reached up to smooth her ponytail. "Why are you staring at me like that, Mom?"

"You look very pale, Tori," Mrs. Carsen said. "Do you feel all right?"

"Of course I feel all right," Tori said. She hated it when her mother hovered over her, treating her like a five-year-old.

"Well, you've got dark circles under your eyes," Mrs. Carsen said. "I wonder if you're coming down with something." She stood up and reached across the table to feel Tori's forehead.

"Mom!" Tori said. She jerked away from her mother's hand. "I told you. I'm fine! I'm just tired— that's all."

"Are you getting enough sleep?" Mrs. Carsen asked.

"She definitely got enough sleep last night," Natalia chimed in from the counter, where she was buttering some toast. "I had to make her get up. I think she would have slept all day!"

Mrs. Carsen peered at Tori again.

But before she could say anything else, Tori spoke up. "So, Mom," she repeated, "can you drive us to the mall?"

"Sure," Mrs. Carsen answered, finally looking away

from Tori. She sipped her coffee. "What about Veronica? Is she going with you?"

Just then Veronica appeared in the doorway. "Am I going where with who?" she asked.

Tori scowled. Veronica Fouchard was the daughter of Roger Arnold's first wife. Veronica had moved in with the Carsens right before Tori's mother married Roger. Tori still wasn't used to having Veronica around. Tori had just turned fifteen, and Veronica had just turned sixteen. Their birthdays were only a few days apart, but their zodiac sign was almost all the girls had in common.

Tori's goal was to go to Nationals and qualify for the Olympics. Veronica's was to wear the latest fashions and make long phone calls to all her friends—every day!

As Veronica strolled into the kitchen and poured herself a cup of coffee, Tori couldn't help thinking that she looked great—as usual. Shiny red highlights glimmered in Veronica's auburn hair. Instead of the casual jeans and sweaters Tori and Natalia wore, Veronica had on a tan knit minidress and thick tights. Her matching short blazer had a wide, pointed collar. She looked as if she had just stepped out of a fashion magazine.

Mrs. Carsen gave Veronica a warm smile. "Tori and Natalia are going to the mall," she explained. "I was asking if you planned to join them."

"No way!" Tori blurted out before Veronica could say anything.

"Tori!" her mother said sharply. "That was rude!"

"Oh, it doesn't matter, Corinne," Veronica said sweetly. "I can't go to the mall, anyway. Betsy and I are going to the library to work on our English papers."

Oh, give me a break! Tori thought. She flashed a quick look at Natalia. Natalia rolled her brown eyes and smirked. They listened as Veronica told Mrs. Carsen about her paper on William Shakespeare.

"I've already read four of his plays," Veronica gushed. "My favorite is *The Tempest*."

Veronica is really laying it on thick, Tori thought. She would bet her best skating dress that Veronica's plans did *not* include going to the library and working on a paper. But, as usual, Veronica was keeping her real plans to herself. She had to! From what Tori could tell, Veronica's plans usually broke at least one of the rules Roger and Corinne had made for the girls. What irked Tori was that Veronica never got caught!

"I always enjoyed Shakespeare when I was in school," Mrs. Carsen said, beaming at Veronica. "I'm very pleased to see you applying yourself."

"Thanks, Corinne," Veronica said. "Living with you and Roger has made a big difference. I've begun to realize how important it is to do my best in school."

This time Tori couldn't help it. She let out a loud snort.

"That's enough, Tori," her mother warned.

"What, Mom?" Tori protested. "I didn't say a thing!" Mrs. Carsen glared at Tori.

As soon as Mrs. Carsen reached down for her coffee, Veronica shot Tori a triumphant smirk.

Tori felt her cheeks redden. It's so unfair, she thought. Veronica gets away with everything! And Mom never budges one inch for me. She gets angry at every little thing I do. If she only knew the real Veronica.

Tori glanced over at her mother. Mrs. Carsen's blond hair was swept back into a ponytail, just like Tori's. She hadn't put on make-up yet, and her skin was as smooth as a teenager's.

Her mother felt Tori's gaze and looked up. Mrs. Carsen's lips softened into a smile. She leaned over and tapped Tori's nose with her middle finger. It was a signal they had made up when Tori was a toddler. It meant "I love you."

Tori felt a deep, powerful rush of love toward her mother. Mom just leans on me because she loves me so much, Tori thought, suddenly feeling happy. I'm *glad* we have such a close relationship. The last thing I'd ever want to do is lie to her the way Veronica does.

3

"**W**hat's taking them so long?" Tori muttered to Natalia.

The two girls were standing in the mall outside Super Sundaes. They were waiting to meet Haley, Martina, and two other Silver Blades members, Nikki Simon and Amber Armstrong. Tori dropped the heavy shopping bag she was carrying for Natalia. It weighed a ton.

"*Boo!*" A pair of hands suddenly covered Tori's eyes. Tori gasped in surprise.

"Guess who?"

"Haley!" Tori ripped Haley's hand off her face and spun around. "You scared me!" She gave Haley a light punch on the arm.

"Sorry," Haley said, giggling. "I couldn't resist."

Nikki, Amber, and Martina strolled over to Tori and Natalia.

"Hey, Tori! We told Haley not to scare you," Nikki said. "But you know Miss Practical Joker. She can't help herself."

"Don't remind me," Tori pretended to grumble.

Nikki grinned and her braces showed. The fourteen-year-old skated pairs in Silver Blades with her partner, Alex Beekman.

Martina pointed to the window of the ice-cream shop. "It's getting crowded in there. Let's grab one of the big booths before they're all taken."

"Okay." Tori picked up the shopping bag and followed her friends into the bustling restaurant. She held the heavy bag in front of her so that it wouldn't knock into anyone's chair.

As Tori got near the booth Martina had chosen, she stumbled. She felt herself pitch forward. She grabbed a small table to break her fall. Silverware and china clattered on the tabletop.

A gray-haired woman sitting at the table reached for Tori's arm and steadied her. Diners nearby stopped talking and looked in Tori's direction. Tori wanted to sink into the floor.

"Are you all right, dear?" the elderly woman asked.

"I'm fine, thank you," Tori mumbled, feeling her cheeks turn red. "Sorry about that."

Conversation at the nearby tables started up again as Tori walked toward the booth. Her heart was pounding. Her left leg had given out on her! Just the way it had at the rink yesterday. And her left foot felt weak.

Tori's mind raced as she slid into the booth.

"Did you leave anything in Canady's for anybody else, Nat?" Haley was saying.

Natalia blushed. "I left a few things," she said. "But I am coming back Wednesday. There is going to be a big sale on winter clothes."

"Aaagh!" Haley faked a horrified look.

Tori glanced under the table to find an empty spot to set down Natalia's bag. But when she tried to release the handles, her fingers wouldn't let go.

"Ow!" Tori yelped. Her fingers were so stiff, she couldn't uncurl them. Her friends looked at her, startled.

"What's the matter, Tori?" Martina asked.

"It's my hand . . . ," Tori murmured. She raised her hand and opened her fingers. Slowly she tried to make a fist.

"Did you hurt it at practice yesterday?" Nikki asked.

"No. . . ." Tori frowned. "It feels stiff, but I don't remember injuring it."

Amber looked at Tori's fingers. "They look okay," she said.

Tori nodded as she flexed her hand. "It feels better now," she said. "Much better." She took a deep breath. Her hand was fine.

"Your hand probably hurts from carrying that shopping bag," Amber said, smiling. "Next time make Natalia carry her own stuff."

"That's right," Haley chimed in. "And Nat, you have to control yourself. From now on, you can only buy seven of everything you see—okay?"

Natalia giggled. "Some of the things are for Jelena," she explained. Jelena was Natalia's older sister—an equally talented figure skater. She still lived with their grandmother back in Russia. "I bought a few things for my grandmother too," Natalia added. "I figured it would make Grandmother feel better. You know, because I can't skate at Nationals."

The girls were all quiet for a second. Natalia had found out recently that she wasn't eligible to perform in the competition. Her father had tried to pull some strings, but it hadn't made a difference. Natalia wasn't a U.S. citizen. Only U.S. citizens could compete to become the U.S. national champion. Natalia had been bitterly disappointed. But she had no choice. She had to follow the rules.

Natalia planned to travel to Philadelphia to watch Tori skate her long program at Nationals. But she would be spending the week before that with her father in Washington, D.C.

Tori thought she knew why Natalia didn't want to stay with her at the hotel in Philadelphia for the week. It would have made Natalia too sad to stand on the sidelines, watching Tori practicing and getting ready for the competition.

Haley waved at the overflowing bags around Natalia's feet.

"I never thought I'd see someone outshop Tori," Haley said, trying to lighten the mood. She grinned at Natalia.

"Excuse me?" Tori cut in. "I can *still* outshop Natalia with one arm tied behind my back." Tori put her elbows on the table and rested her chin in her hands. "I just wasn't trying today. I'm too tired."

"You're *always* tired lately," Haley said. She knocked one of Tori's elbows off the table. Tori forced herself to grin. But it was true.

Tori noticed that Natalia wasn't laughing.

"Haley's right," Natalia told Tori. "You've been tired since you started getting ready for Nationals."

Tori frowned and gulped some of her water. She had expected her mother to bug her about looking pale and tired. But now Natalia was making a federal case out of it too.

Tori saw Amber peering at her, wide-eyed. Amber was only twelve and she worshipped Tori. But she was also one of the most fantastic and naturally talented skaters in Silver Blades. She had placed higher than Tori at Sectionals, the competition that had qualified them both for Nationals. Suddenly Tori felt defensive.

"*Everybody* in Silver Blades is *always* tired," Tori finally told Natalia. She looked around the table at the other girls. "I mean, we have to get up at the crack of dawn six days a week, right?"

No one said anything.

"Maybe you have mono or something," Nikki finally suggested.

"What's mono?" Amber asked.

"Mononucleosis. It's this sickness that makes you tired," Nikki explained. "My cousin had it. She fell asleep in school a couple of times, so her mom took her to the doctor. He said rest was the only real cure. She had to stay in bed for two and a half weeks!"

Tori felt a stab of worry. Mono would make her tired—and she *was* tired. But she couldn't afford to miss a single practice—let alone stay in bed for two and a half weeks!

"You'd feel sick if you had mono," Nikki offered. "You get a cold or the flu or something with it."

"Maybe you just need to take vitamins," Haley suggested. "Or try drinking supershakes. I'll give you my recipe for banana and lecithin."

"Lecithin! Yuck!" Tori wrinkled up her nose.

"And I'm sure Dan could give you tips about feeling more rested," Martina added.

"No way." Tori shook her head firmly. "I'm not saying a word to Dan about feeling tired. He'd probably tell me to eat seaweed for extra energy or visualize myself floating around on a raft in a sea of honey."

Her friends nodded. Dan was a nice guy, but he used pretty strange coaching techniques. He always told Tori to "feel the music" when she skated. He made her practice deep-breathing exercises. And he talked about things like "positive images."

Tori was relieved when the waitress arrived to take their orders. She didn't want to talk about how tired she was anymore.

After the waitress tucked her pad away and walked off, Natalia described Veronica's outfit from that morning.

"If you think I'm obsessed with clothes, you should see Veronica's closet," Natalia said, tucking a strand of her long brown hair back into her bun. "She has more clothes than anyone I know—even Tori."

Tori rolled her eyes. "Yeah. And if I have to hear about how her mother's 'Parisian tailor' made all her clothes one more time, I'll scream," Tori said. "You guys should have heard Veronica giving Natalia a hard time this morning about shopping at Canady's."

"I like Canady's," Amber said.

"We all know Veronica is a snob when it comes to clothes," Natalia said. "But"—she flashed a guilty look in Tori's direction—"I still like her. She really livens things up at home."

"You mean she makes me look bad," Tori said, scowling. "You guys should have heard her latest snow job on my mom. She couldn't come to the mall today because she's at the library. Working on a paper."

All the girls burst out laughing.

"And your mom believed it?" Nikki said.

"Yup. And we all know Veronica is not going to the library," Tori replied.

"I wonder what she is doing," Haley piped up.

Just then the waitress brought a tray loaded with yogurt sundaes and ice cream. The table was suddenly quiet as everyone dug into their treats.

Tori picked up her spoon with her left hand and scooped up some strawberry yogurt. She slipped her right hand under the table and cautiously tested each of her fingers. They still felt stiff.

She thought back to yesterday's practice. She remembered how she'd fallen while she was chasing Haley. Maybe she had hurt her hand then. But she had fallen because her leg gave out. Why did *that* happen? And why had her leg given out ten minutes ago while she was walking across the restaurant?

Tori looked up and saw Natalia watching her. She flashed her friend a bright smile. But it felt unnatural. She didn't feel like smiling.

Nikki leaned across Haley and tapped Tori's arm. "So, how's the new routine?"

"Good," Tori said. She played with the scrunchie holding back her hair. "My long program was great yesterday. I nailed both triple-triples. Usually the second combination is a killer, because I'm tired by then. But yesterday everything just clicked, you know?"

Amber licked her vanilla cone. "I was watching you. It made me want to put two triple-triple jumps in my program, too."

"Watch out," Tori joked. "You're not supposed to skate better than me." Amber giggled.

"Tori, it's going to be so cool when you win the gold at Nationals," Haley said.

"I'll be at Nationals, too," Amber said. "And I beat Tori at Sectionals, so I bet I'll—"

Haley reached out and clapped a hand over Amber's mouth. The older girls often treated Amber like a pesky little sister, even though it annoyed her.

"As I was saying . . ." Haley turned back to Tori, her hand still over Amber's mouth. "Can you imagine the look on Carla Benson's face when you come in first and Amber comes in second?"

Tori smiled. Carla was a fantastic skater. But she was also a snob and a show-off. She roomed with one of Tori's closest friends, Jill Wong, at the International Ice Academy in Colorado. Jill would also be skating at Nationals. Tori couldn't wait to see her.

For a minute Tori imagined herself standing on the winners' platform, beaming with pride as thousands of fans tossed long-stemmed roses at her feet. Carla was frowning up at her from the third-place spot on the podium. An official placed a gleaming gold medal around Tori's neck. Carla frowned harder. Tori smiled dreamily. If her practices continued to go as well as yesterday's, her dream could come true—in less than four weeks.

"Hey, Tori!" Haley said, snapping her fingers.

Tori shook her head and smiled. "Sorry, Haley," she said. "I was just imagining that look on Carla's face!"

A short while later, Tori led the way back into the mall. She pointed in the direction of the health-food store, remembering Haley's suggestion. "Do you guys

mind coming with me while I pick up some vitamins?''

"Sure," Amber agreed cheerfully. The others nodded, and together they started down the mall. As they
stopped to look at a necklace in a jewelry store window, Tori felt an elbow in her side.

"Tor, look," Natalia said quietly. "Isn't that Veronica?" She nodded in the direction of a couple walking
on the other side of the mall fountain.

Tori followed Natalia's gaze. Sure enough, the girl
with the auburn hair was Veronica. But she wasn't
wearing the knit dress she'd had on this morning. She
had changed into a pair of low-slung jeans. Even
though it was winter, Veronica's supertight green-and-
black sweater showed her midriff. A tall boy in a black
leather jacket was walking close to her.

"Is that Veronica's boyfriend?" Amber asked.

"Shhh! It sure looks that way," Tori whispered. She
studied the boy more closely. His long black hair was
pulled into a ponytail. He had high cheekbones and
brown eyes. And he was definitely several years older
than Veronica.

"He's sort of cute," Natalia whispered.

"*Cute?*" Tori echoed doubtfully. "He looks a little
rough to me. Besides, my mother and Roger would go
ballistic if they knew Veronica was dating an older
guy."

Tori kept her eyes on the couple as they strolled
down the mall. The boy reached out and wrapped his

arm around Veronica's waist. She leaned against him. They stopped farther on, to look at the parakeets in the window of Pretty Bird Pet Shop. Tori inhaled sharply. On the back of the boy's jacket was a painting of a snake weaving through a human skull. The snake was poised to strike.

Whoa, Tori thought. She had wondered why Veronica lied so often to Roger and Mrs. Carsen about where she was going and whom she was with. Now Tori knew why she acted so secretive.

Veronica's boyfriend was obviously bad news.

4

Tori studied herself in the mirror in the Silver Blades locker room Wednesday morning. Then she leaned in close and dabbed some concealer under one eye. She put some under the other eye and blended it in. She stood back to survey her work.

Good, she thought. The dark circles were gone. As she hurried out to the rink, she still felt exhausted. But at least no one could see the bags under her eyes.

After her stretches, Tori stepped onto the ice and stroked slowly around the rink. There was a knot in her right calf muscle. Maybe she hadn't stretched it long enough before getting on the ice. She raised her right leg a few inches off the ice and pressed down with her heel.

"Ouch," she muttered. It was really tight. She finished her warm-up, but the leg still felt cramped and painful.

"Morning, Tori!" Dan's voice broke into her thoughts from halfway across the rink. "Are you ready to start?"

"Yes, sir, Coach Dan," Tori called. She skated over to him and gave him a mock salute.

"Great." Dan smiled warmly at her. "You're going to nail both of your triple-triple combinations today, right?"

"Right," Tori said firmly. She pointed to her head. "I've already nailed them up here."

One of the techniques Dan often used was visualization. He was always asking his students to picture themselves skating perfectly. Tori had thought it was ridiculous at first. How could she improve her skating by thinking about it? But it turned out that imagining herself doing her routine flawlessly helped.

But Tori knew she had to *skate* the routine flawlessly too! She wanted to skate her long program perfectly today. Even though she was tired, she knew she could do it.

"Let's take it from the beginning of the footwork," Dan said. "And remember, you need speed *and* strength for the second triple-triple. So pace yourself, okay?"

Tori ran through her program smoothly—until it was time for her first triple-triple combination. As she started the first jump, she could tell instantly that she didn't have enough speed for the entire combination. She managed the first triple toe loop, but she turned the second one into a single toe loop.

"Let's run through it again." Dan's voice traveled across the ice. "You didn't get enough height on the first triple toe loop. That's why you had to bail on the second one. And remember to keep those arms tucked in. But it was a nice try."

Tori grimaced. Dan didn't believe in screaming at his skaters. But she knew "nice try" from Dan was an insult.

She built up speed and tried again. She didn't rotate far enough on the second triple toe loop, and she landed on her bottom and skidded across the ice.

Without saying a word, she stood up and started skating again. She took off for the jump combination, but she bobbled the landing and her hands touched the ice.

Tori tried the jump combination again. And again. She wasn't even getting close. In fact, the harder she tried, the worse she skated.

Finally she glided over to Dan, biting her lower lip in frustration.

Dan studied her, his forehead creased in a frown. "I'm not seeing a strong energy flow here," he said. "You look sluggish. Are you feeling all right?"

"Yes," Tori said. She wasn't surprised that Dan didn't see any energy flow. She was dead on her feet. But she wasn't about to admit that to her coach.

She picked at a sequin on her green skating dress, then smoothed it down with her fingers. Dan watched her quietly for a moment.

"What's up, Tori?" he finally said.

"Nothing," she mumbled.

"Okay," Dan went on patiently. "Maybe I'm way off here, but it looks like your heart isn't in your practice this morning. I don't see your usual enthusiasm coming through."

"I'm working as hard as I can," Tori insisted.

"Quite frankly, I'm not seeing that," Dan went on. "I'm not talking about technical performance. I'm talking about attitude."

Dan spoke gently, but his words stung.

"I really am trying," Tori repeated. "Honest."

Her shoulders slumped. Her skates felt heavy, as if someone had poured concrete in them. Her whole body felt heavy. As hard as she was fighting her tiredness, it wasn't working.

Dan continued watching her face without saying anything. Tori wanted to tell him the truth, but she was afraid. If she told Dan how bad she felt, he'd be on the phone to her mother in no time.

"I'm just a little tired, that's all," she blurted out.

"Have you been getting enough sleep?"

Tori sighed. She was tired of people asking her that!

"Yes, Dan. I go to bed at nine every single night. You know that."

"All right." Dan smiled and put an arm around her

shoulders. "Come on, champ. Let's see a little life out there. I know you can do it. I've seen it before."

Tori forced a smile. "I'll try," she said.

But no amount of trying could give her the spark she lacked. The rest of the practice was as bad as the beginning.

"Okay, Tori," Dan finally called. "Let's call it quits for today." She skated toward him. "Get a good rest tonight," he went on. "I want you tucked into bed at eight-thirty. Got it?"

"Got it," Tori said glumly.

"And don't worry about this morning's session," Dan added. "You'll do better this afternoon, you'll see. And tomorrow you'll be back to your old self, skating brilliantly." He smiled. "Don't let one lousy practice get you down."

Tori forced herself to smile back at him. "Okay," she said. "I won't." But it wasn't just one lousy practice, she thought. It was one lousy practice on top of days and days of feeling tired.

"That's my star!" Dan gave her a thumbs-up and skated off. "See you tomorrow!" he called back.

Tori sighed and put on her skate guards. She had another ten minutes left in her practice. But there didn't seem to be any point. She walked slowly to the locker room.

Inside, she sank down on a bench by her locker. Without even thinking about it, she reached down and massaged her right calf. It was still very tight. And her right foot felt weak and tired. Hot, angry tears pricked her eyelids and spilled down her cheeks. She couldn't remember ever feeling so exhausted and achy. The tears flowed harder as she leaned back against a locker.

"Tori! What's wrong?" someone said.

Tori looked up, surprised to see Nikki standing there. She quickly wiped away the tears with her palm. "It's nothing. I just had a really bad practice, that's all."

"Oh," Nikki said sympathetically. "What happened? Was Dan giving you a hard time?"

"No." Tori shook her head. "You know what Dan's like. You can fall on your rear end twelve times in a row, and he'll praise you for falling so nicely. He's not like Kathy."

Nikki grimaced and rolled her eyes. Kathy Bart was another Silver Blades coach. Her students sometimes called her Sarge behind her back because she was so tough.

"Thank your lucky stars Kathy's not your coach," Nikki said. "Anyway, so you had a bad practice. Big deal. We all do."

"I know, but . . ." Tori hesitated, not sure how much to tell Nikki. "But I only have three and a half weeks until Nationals," she admitted. "And I can't afford to have a bad practice."

The locker room door swung open, and Martina, Amber, and Haley walked in, chatting excitedly.

Haley took one look at Tori and hurried over. "Are you okay?" she asked. She sat on the bench and put her arm around Tori's shoulders.

Tori nodded. "I just had a bad practice, that's all."

"She's worried that she won't be ready for Nationals," Nikki explained as Amber and Martina sat down near Tori.

"We all have bad practices sometimes," Haley said.

"I know," Tori said. "But this is different." She paused for a second. "I've been taking those vitamins every day. But I'm still *so* tired—*all the time*. I have to do *two* triple-triple combinations in my long program. And today I couldn't even land one." The words tumbled out. Tori was relieved to admit how worried she was.

"I bet you're tired because you're stressed out," Nikki suggested. "I've read that stress can keep you from sleeping well, and you end up tired all day, even if you think you slept okay."

"I've heard that too," Amber put in. "Maybe you should try yoga," she went on. "My mom does it every day. She says it really helps her relax."

Tori started to cheer up a little. Maybe she was feeling more stressed out about Nationals than she'd thought. That meant all she had to do was find a way to relax. If she could just do that, she would be all right.

"Thanks, you guys," she said, smiling. "You're right. I'm just letting every little thing freak me out."

"Uh-oh!" Haley shot up off the bench. "Speaking of freaking out, I just remembered that I have a math test this morning! And if I don't study before school, I'm doomed."

As the other girls drifted off to change into their school clothes, Tori went back to unlacing her skates.

I have to stop putting so much pressure on myself and everything will be fine, she told herself. That's all it is—stress.

But she had put pressure on herself to compete at Regionals, and then at Sectionals. She'd put *a lot* of pressure on herself for those events. And it hadn't made her tired. In fact, it had made her skate better than ever before.

So what was different this time? Nationals is the biggest competition I've ever skated in, Tori thought. That's what's different.

"It's just stress. It's just stress. It's just stress." She repeated it to herself over and over.

But as she stood up and stuffed her skates into her bag, she knew in her heart that it was more than that.

5

Two days later, Tori dropped her backpack on a small table at the back of the library and sat down with a sigh. Mrs. Colby, her English teacher, had sent the class to the library to work on an assignment about poetry.

Tori normally would have joined one of the groups of kids sitting at the front of the library, but not today. She was determined to get down to work. The more she got done now, the less homework she would have tonight. And the less homework she had tonight, the earlier she could get to bed. She knew she needed sleep, badly.

She'd been following Dan's advice for the past two nights. She'd been going to bed at eight-thirty, but she still felt exhausted. Her practices hadn't improved, either. She hadn't gotten through the two triple-triple jumps since last weekend, and her feet and legs felt heavy and tight all the time.

She pulled a book of romantic poetry from the shelves, then flipped it open to the middle and started to read.

Before long the words blurred before her eyes. She was so sleepy. She shook her head to clear her vision, then started reading again. And again the words blurred and swam on the page. She propped her head up with her hand and blinked.

Come on, Tori, concentrate, she told herself.

But the words still danced in front of her eyes. Finally she folded her arms and put her head down on the table. I'll rest for just a minute, she thought. Then I'll feel better.

The next thing she knew, someone was gently shaking her shoulder. "Tori?"

Tori bolted upright. Ms. Callahan, the librarian, was at her side. "Are you all right?" she asked, looking down at Tori with concern.

Tori gave her head a little shake, trying to clear it.

"I'm okay," she said quietly. She glanced around to see if any of her classmates had noticed that she'd fallen asleep. She reached up and smoothed down her hair, hoping it wasn't sticking straight up.

"Sorry," she told Ms. Callahan. "I guess I dropped off for a minute. I didn't mean to, really." She checked her watch, surprised to see that it was ten-fifteen. She'd slept for forty-five minutes! English class was nearly over.

Hadn't Nikki's cousin—the one with mono—fallen asleep in school?

Tori quickly stacked her books and stood up.

She grabbed the poetry book and waved it at the librarian.

"I guess I'd better go check this out," she said. "I didn't get much done." She gave an embarrassed little laugh.

"It's all right," Ms. Callahan said. "But I think you'd better see the nurse before you go to your next class. You look a little pale. Maybe you're coming down with something."

"Really, I'm okay," Tori protested. "I was just a little tired, that's all."

"I still think you should see the nurse," Ms. Callahan said firmly.

Tori shrugged. "All right," she said. So she'd be a little late for chemistry. No big deal.

A few minutes later, she was sitting on a chair in the nurse's office with a thermometer in her mouth. Mrs. Sumner slid the thermometer out and read it. "Well, you don't have a fever," she said. She studied Tori for a minute, her blue eyes concerned. "You do look exhausted, though. Have you been getting enough sleep?"

There was that question again!

"I sleep. But it never seems like enough," Tori blurted out before she could stop herself.

Mrs. Sumner nodded sympathetically. "I can imagine," she said. "You keep a very busy schedule with

your skating. It's very exciting that you're going to Nationals, though. We're all pulling for you."

"Thanks," Tori said. At the mention of Nationals,
her heart skipped a beat. Mrs. Sumner would probably watch Nationals on TV. So would dozens—maybe
hundreds or thousands—of other people from Seneca
Hills.

"Have you been feeling this tired for long?" Mrs.
Sumner asked.

"Uh . . ." Tori hesitated. "I'm not sure when it
started," she said finally.

"Hmmm," Mrs. Sumner murmured. "Any swollen
glands?" She put her fingers on Tori's neck and
pressed gently.

"No," Tori said. "I don't think so."

"I don't feel anything." Mrs. Sumner took her
hands away. "Is your throat sore?"

"No. That means I don't have mono, right?" Tori
asked anxiously.

"Let's say it's not likely," Mrs. Sumner answered.
"It is possible, though. You should have a blood test,
just to rule it out. We wouldn't want you skating with
mono. You'll just make yourself sicker. Do you want
me to call your mother?"

"No!" Tori jumped up, alarmed. She couldn't let
Mrs. Sumner tell her mother about this. Mrs. Carsen
would make Tori go to a doctor. And if she did have
mono, the doctor might force her to stay in bed.

"I'll, um, I'll tell her myself," Tori said. "You'd probably have a hard time reaching her, anyway. She's usually in meetings all day because of her design business."

"All right," Mrs. Sumner said. "Just be sure to tell her."

"I will," Tori said. Tori crossed her fingers behind her back. She knew it was a babyish thing to do. But it made her feel better. Because she wasn't sure she *would* tell her mother. Even if she did have mono, she knew she could last long enough to skate at Nationals. After that she could lie in bed for *three* weeks if she had to.

"Do you feel well enough to go back to class, Tori?" Mrs. Sumner asked.

Tori frowned. "I don't know," she said.

"Do you have any tests today?" the nurse asked.

"No," Tori said.

"Then why don't you go home and go to bed?" Mrs. Sumner suggested. She reached for the pad of dismissal forms on her desk. She jotted Tori's name on one. "Is there someone who can pick you up?"

"I can call my stepfather," Tori said.

"All right."

Tori picked up the phone, thinking fast. As soon as the answering machine picked up, she began talking. "Hi, Roger? It's Tori. I'm in the nurse's office. I wasn't feeling well in English, and she thinks I should go home. Can you come get me?" Tori talked right over Roger's voice on the outgoing message as he announced that no one was able to come to the phone. Then she hung up before the beep, knowing her voice hadn't been recorded.

"Okay," Tori said to Mrs. Sumner. "He's going to pick me up out front in a few minutes."

"Good. Bring this back with your mother's signature when you come to school tomorrow. And try to get some rest, Tori." Mrs. Sumner handed Tori the pink dismissal slip.

"Sure. Thanks, Mrs. Sumner." Tori gathered her things and put on her jacket. She went to her locker to collect her skate bag and more schoolbooks. Then she headed out the front door toward the stop where she could catch the city bus home. She couldn't wait to crawl into her cozy bed.

It was only two blocks to the bus stop, and the first bus came right away. Tori climbed on and dropped her money in the coin slot. As she took her seat, she got a nervous feeling in her stomach.

I'm forgetting something, but what? she thought. Then it hit her. Haley's mother was supposed to drive Haley and Tori from school to skating practice later today. Tori had to find a way to get Mrs. Arthur to pick her up at home.

With a stab of guilt, she realized that she'd also have to get around having her mother sign the dismissal slip.

Suddenly Tori remembered that Veronica had forged her mother's signature before. If Veronica can get away with it, Tori thought, so can I.

Tori's conscience nagged at her, but she ignored it. I don't have a choice, she reminded herself firmly. If I tell Mom that I fell asleep in school and got sent to the nurse, she'll totally overreact. She'll make me see a doctor.

When the bus reached her stop, Tori got off and trudged toward home. She pulled her collar tightly around her neck in the frigid air. Her backpack and skate bag grew heavier by the minute, making the ten-minute walk seem endless.

She used her key to let herself in. The silent house had never seemed so welcoming. She couldn't wait to fall into her soft bed and pull her down comforter up to her ears.

She headed up the stairs, then stopped short.

Upstairs, from a room down the hall, she heard someone talking on the phone.

Oh, no! Tori thought with dread. Mom's home!

6

Tori turned and started running down the stairs.

Before she reached the front door, a voice shouted, "Hey!"

Tori whirled around. It wasn't her mother. It was Veronica! "What are *you* doing here?" Tori demanded.

"*Me?* What about you?" Veronica tossed her hair. "Don't tell me that Miss Goody Two-Shoes is cutting school?"

"No, I'm *not* cutting school," Tori said, mimicking Veronica's tone. "I don't do things like that."

"Oh, that's right," Veronica said. "You're too dull to break any rules."

Tori gave her a cold stare. "I wouldn't call it dull, Veronica. I'd call it smart."

"Oh, yeah, *real* smart," Veronica said. "Let's face it, Tori. All you ever do is go to school and skate."

Tori fumed. "Maybe that isn't your idea of fun," she said, putting her hands on her hips, "but I work really hard. And it's gotten me all the way to Nationals. And it'll get me to the Olympics, too. And that's more than you'll ever be able to say."

Veronica smirked. "It hasn't done much for your social life, though, has it?"

"Oh, as if your social life is something to brag about," Tori retorted.

Veronica stared at her.

"I saw you at the mall last weekend," Tori went on. "Maybe I should tell Mom and Roger that you were with that older guy when you were supposed to be at the library with Betsy."

A smile formed on Veronica's lips as she leaned against the door frame. "It's my word against yours, Tori," she said smoothly. "Go ahead and be a little tattletale."

Tori flushed.

"How about when I tell her that you cut school today?" Tori tried again. "All she has to do is call the school office."

Veronica laughed. "Go ahead. Tell her. And be sure to tell her how you knew. Tell her you were cutting school, too."

"I already told you," Tori bluffed. "I had permission to come home."

"Oh, really?" Veronica said. She put a finger on her chin and pretended to think for a minute. "Hmmm. Then I wonder why you were running away like a scared baby rabbit when you thought I was your mother?''

Tori glared at her. She couldn't think of anything to say. Veronica had her.

"So you won't tell on me, and I won't tell on you," Veronica said. "Right?"

"All right," Tori grumbled. "Just this one time."

Tori felt a stab of guilt. The last thing she wanted was to be like Veronica—sneaking around, hiding things, and lying all the time.

Just the other day, Tori had been so grateful that she didn't have to lie to her mother! Now she was lying to the school nurse and trying to figure out how she could forge her mother's signature on a dismissal slip.

"Why are you cutting school, anyway?" Veronica asked.

"I fell asleep in the library and the nurse sent me home," Tori snapped. "But I don't want Mom to know that. She'd make a big deal out of it and take me to the doctor's."

"Really? Bummer," Veronica said. "That kind of figures, though. Corinne is so picky."

"She's *not* picky," Tori said. "She just worries about me. But I don't want her to start blowing things out of proportion. I have to concentrate on Nationals right now."

Tori paused, not sure why she had bothered to explain things to Veronica. But, to Tori's surprise, Veronica was listening intently, as if she were really interested.

"I've seen your mom freak out when she thinks you look pale, or tired, or something," Veronica said thoughtfully.

"Exactly," Tori said. "If Mom knew that the nurse sent me home today, she'd put me to bed and feed me chicken soup for a week. I just wanted to come home—on my own—and get some sleep without her blowing it up into a huge deal."

Veronica burst out laughing. "Hey, Tori, you're starting to think like me—what your mom doesn't know won't hurt her!"

"No, I'm not starting to think like you," Tori said defensively. "I just didn't have a choice today, that's all."

"Whatever," Veronica said, grinning.

"Fine," Tori mumbled. "Think what you want." As she started toward her room, she remembered the dismissal slip. She turned back to Veronica.

"You can forge my mother's signature, can't you?"

Veronica cocked her head. "Sure," she said. "Why?"

"I have to have the dismissal slip from the nurse signed." She unzipped her backpack and rummaged through it until she found the pink slip and a pen. She handed both to Veronica.

"No problem." Veronica signed the note and gave it back. "Now you owe me one," she said.

"Okay," Tori conceded. "Thanks." She studied the signature. It was good—so good that even Tori would have believed her mother had signed it. The nurse would never suspect a thing. Tori felt another wave of guilt wash over her. She had never forged her mother's signature or skipped school. She had always felt as if she could tell her mother anything.

But it was different this time. Now Tori was old enough to skate for herself. She wasn't going to Nationals to live out her mother's dreams. It was *Tori's* dream. She wanted to win Nationals more than anything. That was all she could worry about now. Even if it meant she had to sleep during the school day and then lie about it.

Tori slipped the note into her pocket and headed for her room. She crawled into bed. Ten minutes later, she was sound asleep.

Later that afternoon, Tori's alarm woke her with a start. She rolled out of bed and yawned. As she stretched her arms over her head, then reached down to touch her toes, she could tell that the heavy tiredness had eased up. She bounced on her toes. Suddenly she was dying to be on the ice.

She pulled on her black tights and slipped into the black-and-white flowered minidress she'd worn to school. She remembered that she had to call Haley's mom to see if she could pick her up at home.

As Tori walked down the hall, she realized that Veronica was on the phone again inside her room.

Tori tapped lightly on Veronica's door, then stuck

her head in. "I need the phone," she said. "Right away."

Veronica put her hand over the receiver of the cordless phone and spoke to Tori. "Just a minute."

"Okay. But make it quick," Tori demanded.

Veronica rolled her eyes and turned her back on Tori. She talked on as though Tori hadn't said a word. Tori stood in the doorway, tapping her fingernails on the door frame until Veronica finally said good-bye. As she turned around to hand the cordless phone to Tori, Tori was startled to see her smiling. She'd thought Veronica would be mad at her for making her hang up. Instead, Veronica's eyes glowed with happiness.

I'd bet anything she was talking to a boy, Tori thought, smiling a little.

Tori took the phone and quickly dialed Haley's number. She paced up and down the hallway, counting the rings as she tried to figure out what to say to Haley's mom.

The answering machine picked up. Tori punched the Off button on the phone before the message had even finished. She sat down at the top of the stairs to wait before trying again.

Five minutes later, she dialed again. The machine answered again. Tori put her feet on the step below her, impatiently jiggling her legs up and down to shake out the tightness in her muscles. Five more minutes passed; then Tori tried again. No good. She glanced at her watch and felt a wave of panic. What if

Haley's mother was out? What if she went straight to school to pick up Haley and Tori?

Tori tried one more time. "Come on, please, please, please," she muttered. The machine answered, and Tori punched the Off button, hard. "Darn, darn, darn," she said. She heard footsteps in the hall and looked up to see Veronica standing next to her.

"Something wrong?" Veronica asked.

"I'm trying to get a ride to the rink," Tori answered. "I was going to ask Haley's mom to pick me up here, but she's not home."

"And you can't call Corinne or Roger?"

"Exactly," Tori said. "And I don't have time to take the bus back to school to get my ride." She groaned. "I'm dead, that's all. Just dead."

"Well," Veronica said, "I think I might be able to help you out."

"Really?" Tori perked up. "You mean you could get me a ride?"

"Sure," Veronica said. "I know someone who drives."

Veronica had only lived in Seneca Hills for a few months, but she'd already made a lot of friends. One was a girl named Samantha who had her driver's license, Tori remembered.

Veronica would get her own license later this year. Mrs. Carsen planned to give her driving lessons after the weather warmed up.

Veronica picked up the phone and punched in a number. She said hi and then explained Tori's problem. "How soon do you need to go?" Veronica asked Tori.

"As soon as possible," Tori said. "My practice is at two-thirty."

Veronica relayed the information and said good-bye.

"That was easy," she told Tori. "Your ride will be here in ten minutes."

"Wow! Thanks a lot, Veronica," Tori said gratefully. She let out a huge sigh of relief. Then she hurried to get ready.

I hate to admit it, Tori thought, *but some of Veronica's wild habits are actually starting to come in handy.*

Tori left a message for Haley at school saying she'd meet her at the rink. She'd figure out what to say to Haley and Mrs. Arthur later. Tori put on her Silver Blades jacket, then went down to the foyer to wait for Samantha.

A few seconds later, Veronica bounded down the stairs dressed in a short skirt and a fuzzy neon green sweater with navy blue stripes. Tori noticed that she'd also put on pale pink lipstick.

"You're coming too?" Tori asked, surprised.

"Of course," Veronica answered. She peered out the window by the front door. "Okay. He's here," she said. "Let's go."

"He?" Tori repeated, following Veronica outside. "But I thought . . ." Her words trailed off as she spotted an unfamiliar car, a silver Camaro, idling in

the driveway. Loud rock music blared through the open windows. Tori saw a big scrape along one side of the car, as if it had just been in an accident. Slowly her eyes traveled to the driver's seat, but she'd already guessed who was sitting there—the guy from the mall with the long hair and the ugly leather jacket.

Tori's heart sank. Did Veronica really expect her to get into a car with this guy?

7

Tori stopped short on the walkway and grabbed Veronica's arm. "No way, Veronica," she said. "I'm not taking a ride from your friend."

"What?" Veronica stared at her.

"I thought you called Samantha," Tori explained. "My mother will kill me if I get into that car. I'm not allowed to drive around with boys she doesn't know. And neither are you."

Veronica shook her head in disbelief. "Are you crazy, Tori? Your mother's never going to find out about this. Unless you plan to tell her," she said. She narrowed her eyes.

"No, I'm not going to tell her," Tori said. "But that guy's car has a big dent. And he looks like he's—"

"Come on, Tori," Veronica cut in. "Stop making a fuss over nothing and get in the car. You're going to be late if you don't hurry up."

As Veronica started toward the silver car, Tori stood still for another minute. Finally, reluctantly she followed Veronica over to the driveway. She was furious at Veronica for putting her in this situation. But now she didn't really have a choice. If she didn't want to miss practice, she had to take a ride with Veronica's boyfriend.

It's just one ride, Tori told herself. And we're not going very far.

Veronica slid into the front seat. As Tori climbed into the backseat, the motor revved loudly.

Tori sank down into her seat, praying that none of the neighbors had spotted her climbing into the car.

"Hey, Veronica." The boy behind the wheel leaned over and kissed her on the cheek. Then he turned around to look at Tori. "Hi. It's Tori, right?" he asked. He took off his dark sunglasses and gave Tori a lopsided grin.

"Evan, Tori," Veronica said. "Tori, this is Evan."

"Hi," Tori mumbled unhappily. As she looked at Evan, she noticed three gold hoops hanging from his right ear. She also noticed something else—he was even older than she'd thought!

"So do you go to, um, Seneca Hills High?" she asked, trying to find out more about him.

Evan laughed. "Not anymore. I'm a sophomore at the J.C."

A sophomore at the junior college? Tori thought. "Seneca Hills Junior College?" she blurted out.

"Yup," Evan said cheerfully.

Tori couldn't believe it. Evan had to be at least twenty!

Evan put his sunglasses back on. He backed the car out of the driveway and onto the street. "Veronica said you needed a ride to the rink?"

"Yes," Tori said.

"No problem," Evan replied. "I used to play hockey a lot. I know exactly where it is."

As they drove along the streets of her neighborhood, Tori was glad that the windows of Evan's car were tinted. The last thing she needed was for one of the neighbors to spot her in the back of a car being driven by a college sophomore! If her mother got wind of it, she'd throw a fit!

Up front, Veronica and Evan seemed to forget all about Tori. Evan cranked up the volume on the stereo again. The two of them sang loudly to the rock music.

Ten minutes later, they were a block from the rink. Suddenly Tori realized that she'd better not let Evan drop her off right in front. What if Haley's mother, or another parent, was there and saw her getting out of the car?

When they stopped at the next red light, Tori tapped Evan on the shoulder.

He turned down the radio and looked at her. "Yeah?"

"I can just get out here," Tori said. She grabbed her skate bag and reached for the door handle.

"I can take you the rest of the way," Evan said.

Veronica grinned. "I don't think Tori wants to

get caught with us, Evan. Her mommy might find out she was cutting school and riding around with boys."

"I wasn't cutting, Veronica!" Tori tried to protest. But Veronica and Evan were laughing too loudly to hear her.

"That's okay, Tori," Evan said. He gave her a knowing wink. "We'll see you later."

Exasperated, Tori opened the door. She grabbed her skate bag and slid out of the car. "Thanks for the ride, Evan," she said.

"Hey, no problem," he replied. "Anything to help Veronica's little stepsister."

Tori's mouth dropped open. At first she wanted to argue with Evan. But over what? she thought. She *was* Veronica's stepsister. Sort of. And she *was* younger.

And Veronica had been nice enough to get her a ride. It was practically the first kind thing the girl had ever done for her.

Tori hesitated for just a second before she glanced at Veronica. "Thanks," she said.

Veronica smiled. Tori had to blink. That wasn't Veronica's usual sarcastic grimace. It was an actual, honest-to-goodness smile! And it was aimed at Tori!

When Tori arrived at the rink, she was surprised—and relieved—to discover that the locker room and the ice were empty.

She checked her watch. No wonder no one was here—she was early. If I hurry, I can be the first one out on the ice, she thought. She might even have enough time to run through her long program before practice officially began.

She quickly changed into a bright pink skating dress and her skates. She put her hair in a ponytail and tied a ribbon around it, her fingers flying. Then she hurried out to the ice to begin loosening up.

When she was finished with her warm-up, she skated over to the music booth and put in her tape. She returned to center ice and struck her opening pose. The first strains of the dramatic music from the opera *Faust* filled the rink. Tori closed her eyes and counted the first few beats. Then she began her routine with the footwork that led into her first jump, a double axel.

Tori felt focused, calm, and centered. For the first time in weeks, her tired feeling dropped away completely. She flew through her spins and jumps with grace and power. It was almost as though the music itself were carrying her through every move. Even both triple-triple combinations were flawless.

Tori couldn't remember the last time skating had felt this easy and good.

This is the way it's supposed to feel, she thought, striking her closing pose. Her heart pounded furiously as she bowed to an imaginary crowd. In her mind, they were screaming wildly, jumping to their feet, clapping thunderously.

Just then the sound of real applause broke into her thoughts. She pivoted on her skates to see who was watching. Dan skated toward her from the edge of the rink, still clapping.

"Wonderful," he said. "That was beautiful."

"Thanks." Tori felt a rush of pleasure. "I didn't know anyone was watching."

"I didn't think so. It's good to see the old Tori back," he said warmly. "If you skate like that at Nationals, you're sure to come home with a medal."

"I hope so," she said, smiling happily.

Dan told her to keep working on her long program until the other skaters arrived. As she skated back to center ice, she spotted Haley and Natalia heading for the women's locker room.

Haley spotted her too and waved. "Where were you?" she called.

Tori skated over to the boards.

"I got a message at school that you weren't coming with us," Haley said.

"We thought you were sick or something," Natalia said.

Tori shook her head quickly. "I just had a dentist's appointment, that's all." The lie popped out before she even realized what she was saying.

Natalia stared at her. "I didn't know you were going to the dentist today," she said. "You never said anything about it."

"Mom told me about it last week, but I kind of forgot about it until the last minute." Tori could feel her face grow hot.

"So your mom picked you up from school?" Haley asked.

"Actually, Roger picked me up." Suddenly it seemed as if one lie just led to another and another. "Um, and it was too late to go back to school when I was done," she added. "So we just came here."

"Oh." Haley nodded, seeming satisfied. She and Natalia continued on their way to the locker room.

Tori watched them go. Why did you lie? she scolded herself. They're your best friends! They would have understood.

But Tori didn't want her friends to know the truth. Just as she didn't want her mother to know the truth.

Her cheeks still burned as she skated back to center ice.

It's okay, she thought, trying to reassure herself. It's only a little lie. And after today, she wouldn't have to tell any more lies—not to Dan, or her mother, or the school nurse, or her closest friends. Because whatever had been making her feel lousy was finally gone.

She was skating like a champion again.

8

"**H**ere it is!" Haley said. She flipped a page in the large hardcover book in front of her. "Look at this! Isn't this picture funny?" She pushed the book across the table to Tori.

Nikki, Martina, Natalia, and Amber were also squeezed into the booth at the ice rink's snack bar.

It was the following Saturday, right before afternoon practice. Mack, the man who ran the Zamboni, had had trouble starting the huge machine earlier. Now they were waiting for him to finish cleaning the ice.

Tori looked at the glossy photograph in Haley's book. It showed a figure skater doing a very fast spin. Her face was contorted into a strange grimace. Haley crossed her eyes and twisted her lips to one side, trying to imitate the face. Everyone cracked up.

"That's awful," Tori said. "Do you think we really look like that when we're spinning?"

"Probably not. None of us can spin as fast as Cara Hopkins," Nikki pointed out, waving her hand at the picture.

"We'd better," Amber said, "if we want to medal at Nationals."

"Don't remind me," Tori groaned. "She's going to be tough to beat." Tori tried to keep her tone light. But it wasn't easy.

Her triumph from that day last week when she'd skated perfectly had not lasted long. The next day, the same old tired feeling had come back. And so had Tori's fear that there was something seriously wrong with her body.

Some practices were better than others. But even her best performances lately wouldn't be good enough to win her a medal at Nationals. There were days when she wondered if she could skate her program— period. Forget winning, she prayed on those days. Just don't let me humiliate myself in front of the whole country!

I should tell Mom, she thought. What if I have something the doctor can fix with a shot? I might lose at Nationals because I was too stubborn and scared to get a *shot*!

And what if I have mono? she asked herself. Mom would probably let me skate at Nationals anyway. I can always rest afterward.

Or maybe it really is stress. She thought of how perfectly she had skated the past week—when she'd thought she was alone. Maybe the two things were connected.

But a small voice in the back of her head always asked the harder questions: What if you have something way worse than mono? Or too much stress? What if the doctor makes you stop skating right away? You might never get another chance at Nationals!

"Maybe you look like this during your spins, Tor." Haley yanked Tori's sleeve to get her attention. Then she stuck out her tongue and crossed her eyes.

"Or like this!" Amber made the tendons in her neck stand out and stretched her mouth into a grimace.

Tori giggled. Her friends were so goofy.

"Hey, look, Patrick! I think we've stumbled onto the Miss Teenage America contestants."

Tori turned at the sound of his voice. It was Nikki's partner, Alex. He and Haley's partner, Patrick, were walking into the snack bar. They had obviously seen the silly faces the girls were making.

"They sure are pretty," Alex went on.

"Yeah." Patrick joined in the teasing. "Total babes!"

"Hey!" Haley stood up and lightly punched Alex's arm. "Leave us alone."

"No way," Alex said. He and Patrick grabbed chairs from a nearby table and sat down. "Giving you guys a hard time is too much fun."

"I'm not even going to ask what those weird faces were all about," Patrick said.

"Weird faces?" Tori gave him an innocent look.

"What are you talking about? They looked normal to me."

Alex shook his head. "Maybe we don't really want to know," he said, reaching across the table for the book the girls had been looking at. *"Figure Skating: Poetry in Motion,"* he read. "Where did this come from?"

"It's Natalia's," Amber said.

"My dad sent it to me," Natalia explained. "I think he feels guilty that I'm not skating at Nationals. Like it's his fault or something!"

"Cool book," Alex said, flipping through the pages.

"Did you see that photo of Kristi Yamaguchi doing a perfect sit spin?" Haley said, pointing to a full-page photo near the front of the book.

"She's an unbelievable skater," Alex commented.

While her friends leafed through the skating book, Tori grabbed her bottle of mineral water. As she tilted it back to take a sip, the plastic bottle slipped out of her hand. Her grip had gone slack—on its own. It was as if someone else had given her hand the order to drop the bottle!

Tori stared as the bottle bounced off the table and fell into her lap. It flipped end over end. Water splashed on her skating dress.

Alex looked up from the skating book. "Drink much, Tor?" he teased her.

Her other friends laughed, but Tori felt the color drain out of her face.

I couldn't grip the bottle, she thought. It was the opposite of what had happened to her hand before.

Then, she hadn't been able to loosen her grip on Natalia's shopping bag. This felt more like . . . like the way her leg had collapsed at the rink and at Super Sundaes. Tori felt a flash of panic. Did mono make your muscles weak?

She licked her lips, trying to speak.

"It's okay, Tori," Nikki said. She grabbed a handful of paper napkins and started mopping up the table. "It's just water. It'll dry."

"I know," Tori choked out. She made herself smile as she took a handful of napkins from Nikki. She dabbed at her skating dress with her left hand.

While her friends looked at the skating book again, Tori cautiously flexed her right hand. Then she pointed each of her fingers. Then she made a tight fist. It worked, no problem.

But she didn't understand why she had lost her grip on the bottle. It was scary. She sat quietly as everyone else looked at Natalia's book and talked about the pictures.

A few minutes later the group broke up. Mack had finished clearing the ice. Everyone went to the locker rooms to change.

Tori dressed slowly. She didn't feel excited about practice anymore. She decided to work on her spins. She didn't want to even think about her jumps. She felt lousy and tired.

As she came out of a sit spin, she heard a loud cheer from the other end of the rink. Tori glanced over.

"Good job, Amber!" Kathy Bart said. "That's exactly how you're supposed to do it."

Amber was breathing hard and grinning as she skated in small circles around her coach.

"Try it again—just like that," Kathy said.

The small girl skated off and then back toward her coach, gaining speed. She leaped into the air and did a perfect triple toe loop–double loop.

Tori's heart sank. That was me two months ago, she thought. Why can't I skate like that now? Amber was skating really well. And so would the other competitors at Nationals. Maybe it really is stress that's making me sick, Tori thought. Because, boy, am I stressed!

"Tori!"

The voice snapped Tori to attention.

Veronica! What in the world is she doing here? Tori wondered. She looked toward the double doors. Veronica was walking in with Evan. His hands were stuffed inside the pockets of his leather jacket.

Tori skated to the side of the rink and waved.

"Hi," she called. She felt a flicker of worry as Veronica and Evan approached. "Nothing's wrong at home, is it?" she asked.

"Of course not, silly," Veronica said. "Why would anything be wrong?"

Tori shrugged. "You don't usually hang out at the rink."

Veronica smiled sweetly. "We just came to watch you skate."

Tori felt her mouth drop open in surprise. "*You* came to watch *me* skate?" she repeated.

"Sure," Veronica said. "Evan was really interested in seeing your routine."

"Yeah," Evan chimed in. "Veronica told me that you're a good skater, but I didn't realize how good until she said you're going to Nationals. Then I remembered seeing you skate on TV. You're fantastic!"

Tori glowed with pleasure. "Thanks, Evan," she said. As he smiled, she noticed that it made his eyes light up. They were a warm, deep brown—the color of hot chocolate.

No wonder Veronica thinks he's so cute, Tori thought. He *is* cute! And he's nice.

"Evan likes to skate, too," Veronica said, pulling Tori out of her thoughts.

"Really?" Tori looked at him.

"I used to play hockey, Veronica," he said, a sheepish expression on his face. "That's a different kind of skating. I can't even come close to doing the stuff that Tori can do on the ice."

"Why don't you show him your long program, Tori," Veronica said. It was more like an order than a request.

"Okay." Tori laughed. Veronica is too much, she thought. She was suddenly acting as if she were at the rink all the time and totally involved in Tori's skating. All to impress Evan!

"Why don't you guys sit down," Tori added, waving

to the bleachers. "I'll show you some of the best parts."

"That's cool," Evan said, looking pleased. Then he and Veronica sat down to watch.

Tori skated to center ice, glad to have an audience. She waited for a few skaters to move out of her way. Then she started the serpentine pattern of steps from her long program. She launched into a flawless triple Lutz. As she landed the jump cleanly, the music from her program started up inside her head. She glided backward along the ice, letting the music carry her through the routine. Tori performed a triple salchow and followed it up with a layback spin. As she spun rapidly over the ice, she felt light and graceful.

She was skating beautifully, and it felt wonderful. Maybe it was because she was relaxed. Maybe that was the secret, Tori thought. She just needed to do some yoga and do Dan's breathing exercises. And forget about how well everyone else was skating, and whether she'd bomb at Nationals.

Tori began to slow the spin. As she did, she knew right away that something was wrong. The ice beneath her skates was shifting, tilting one way and then another, even after she'd come to a complete stop.

In a panic, she reached out for something to hold on to. But her fingers gripped only the empty air. Her stomach lurched as the white ice suddenly rose up to meet her.

A second later, everything went black.

9

Tori woke up dazed. She didn't know where she was. She was lying on something cold and hard. Voices flew all around her.

"Tori? Tori?" A voice broke through the rest. "Can you hear me, Tori? Are you all right?"

It was Kathy Bart. Tori wanted to answer, but she couldn't get her mouth to work. Her eyelids felt heavy—too heavy to open.

"Get something under her head." That was Kathy again. Tori felt her head being lifted. Something soft was slid under it.

Slowly her mind began to clear. I was spinning, she remembered. And then I fell. I'm lying on the ice at the Seneca Hills arena.

She opened her eyes. Kathy's anxious face looked

down at her. Kathy looked fuzzy, and so did the skaters who surrounded her. Tori could just make out Haley and Martina and a few other kids.

"Hi, guys," Tori murmured. She closed her eyes again.

"Tori?" Kathy said anxiously.

"I'm okay," Tori said. She opened her eyes, and this time everything swam into focus. She put one hand on the ice and slowly pushed herself into a sitting position. She did a mental check of her body. Her feet felt okay—so did her ankles and her arms and everything else. "I'm okay," she said again, this time with more conviction.

"What happened?" Kathy asked. "Did you hit your head when you fell?"

"No, I just . . ." Tori hesitated. "I don't know. . . ."

Kathy looked behind her. "All right, people, let's back off a little here," she said sternly. She extended one arm, as if to push them all back. Several skaters glided slowly away from Tori, but most seemed reluctant to move.

"Come on, folks," Kathy insisted, "the show is over. Go on back to your practicing, please. Rubbernecking will not improve your skating one bit."

Some of the skaters laughed, and the small gathering finally broke up. Natalia, Haley, Nikki, Martina, and Amber stayed nearby. Kathy looked as though she were about to shoo them away, too, but then Natalia spoke up.

"Do you want me to go call Tori's mother?" she suggested.

"No," Tori cried, but no one paid attention to her.

"That's a good idea," Kathy said. "You can use the phone in my office."

"Please don't," Tori said to Natalia. "You really don't need to." Natalia skated off.

"I'm fine," Tori insisted. "Look." She pushed herself to her knees. She paused to make sure she wasn't dizzy. She stood, wobbled, nearly lost her balance, then caught it. Haley reached out to steady her, but Tori waved her off.

Kathy scrambled to her feet, too.

"Can you make it to the bleachers? I think we should get you off the ice," the coach said.

"No problem," Tori said, and pushed off more forcefully than she needed to. She had to prove she really was all right, even though she felt shaky.

"Easy there," Kathy said. "We don't want you going down again."

"I won't," Tori told her, hoping it was true. She skated toward the opening in the boards. Kathy followed her closely. Amber, Haley, Nikki, and Martina skated beside her.

Tori glanced toward the bleachers for Veronica and Evan. She'd been showing off for them when she fainted. Tori felt her cheeks redden. What a great impression she must have made!

"Are you okay?" Veronica asked, walking quickly over to Tori. There was real concern in her eyes.

"What happened?" Evan asked. He put a hand under Tori's elbow to steady her.

"I guess . . ." Tori stalled. Her mind raced to come up with an excuse. "That spin I was doing. I was going superfast, and when I came out of it, I got dizzy. Totally dizzy. But I'm fine now."

"Sit down," Kathy commanded.

Tori obediently walked the few steps to the bleachers. As she sat down, she could feel her fingers trembling and her heart beating furiously.

The fear that had been gnawing at her for the past few weeks was growing to monster size. She tried to push it away, but this time, ignoring it wouldn't work. Something was wrong with her, and she was terrified.

"Mrs. Carsen is on her way," Natalia said, walking over to Tori.

"Great," Tori muttered. "That's all I need."

As Natalia sat down with Tori's other friends, Kathy cleared her throat.

"Hey, you guys," Kathy said. "I'd like it if Amber would get Tori some orange juice from the snack bar. Natalia, you can sit here with Tori. The rest of you should get back to work. Your practice sessions aren't over yet." She sat down next to Tori.

"But Kathy, we're worried about Tori," Haley protested. "We want to make sure she's okay." Nikki and Martina nodded in agreement.

"I didn't realize you'd earned a medical degree, Haley." Kathy smiled. Haley laughed.

"Go on, Haley," Tori urged. "I'm okay. I'll probably be back out there in a few minutes."

Kathy raised her eyebrows but said nothing. Finally Tori's friends skated off. Evan and Veronica sat down on the other side of Tori.

"Are you feeling dizzy now?" Kathy asked.

"No." Tori shook her head firmly to reassure the coach. She wasn't lying—the dizziness and weak feeling had passed. "I'm okay, really. I don't know why I got dizzy, but I'm okay now."

"Tell me, Tori. What have you had to eat today?" Kathy asked.

Tori immediately saw what the coach was getting at—and knew exactly how to reply.

"Hardly anything," she said quickly. "Just an apple and some vanilla yogurt." It wasn't true. She had eaten two good meals already that day, and she wasn't hungry.

"*What?*" Veronica did a double take. "That's not true, Tori. At lunch, I saw you have a—"

Tori silenced Veronica with a glare. "Oh yeah," Tori said quickly. "I had a handful of trail mix, too. Two handfuls, maybe."

Veronica stared back at her, but she stayed silent. Veronica had seen Tori eat a big turkey sandwich and a salad for lunch that day. But Tori didn't want her announcing that to Kathy. If Kathy thought Tori's fainting spell was due to hunger, maybe she'd brush it off as unimportant. But if Kathy didn't know what had caused it, she might stop Tori from skating anymore today.

"Tori," Kathy said sternly. "You know that's not an adequate diet for an athlete in training. What are you trying to do to yourself?"

Tori looked down at her hands, pretending to be embarrassed. "I just wanted to lose a few pounds," she said. "Before Nationals." She looked up and met Kathy's eyes. "I guess I went overboard."

"I told her she was being stupid," Veronica piped up. "When she kept talking about losing weight before Nationals, I told her she was crazy. She wouldn't listen to me."

Kathy studied Veronica, then Tori. "Well, now you know how dangerous it is to train without eating enough food. I want you to just sit here for the rest of practice. Drink the O.J. Amber brings, okay?"

Tori nodded.

As Kathy went over to the boards to talk to Nikki, Tori stood up slowly. She wasn't dizzy, but her calf muscles felt tight—incredibly tight.

"Tori," Veronica said warningly. "What do you think you're doing?"

"I'm going back on the ice," Tori said.

"No way," Veronica said. "Didn't you hear what Kathy said? You're done for the day."

"Veronica's right," Evan chimed in. "You'd better take it easy for a while."

With a frustrated sigh, Tori sank back down.

"I can't believe this," she muttered.

"What?" Evan asked.

"I'm leaving for Nationals in two weeks. If I don't get in enough practices, I'm going to make a fool of myself!" Tori reached down and rubbed her tired calf muscles. She didn't want Veronica and Evan to see that she was trying not to cry.

There was a long silence.

"You're *not* going to make a fool of yourself," Veronica finally said. "I've known you long enough to realize that you're not the type of person who does that."

Just then Tori's mother rushed into the rink.

"Tori! Tori! Are you all right?" Mrs. Carsen shouted. She sounded frantic.

Tori cringed. "I'm fine, Mom," she called back.

Mrs. Carsen hurried over to the bleachers. She looked so pale, Tori thought she might be about to pass out herself. Mrs. Carsen grabbed Tori and hugged her hard, pressing Tori's face against her forest green silk suit.

"Are you sure you're all right?" she asked.

Tori pulled away. "Yes, honest."

Kathy skated up to the boards and then walked toward Tori and her mother.

Mrs. Carsen breathed a deep sigh of relief. "What happened?" she asked, brushing a blond curl off Tori's forehead.

"I was doing a—"

Mrs. Carsen silenced Tori with a wave of her hand. She turned to Kathy. "Tell me everything."

"Tori got dizzy as she was coming out of a spin. She took a nasty tumble," Kathy explained. "We think maybe she just didn't eat enough today."

"What do you mean, she didn't eat enough?" Mrs. Carsen asked sharply. "Tori eats sensibly. She knows how important that is for an athlete."

Uh-oh, Tori thought.

"You're right, Mom," she said quickly. "I do know. But I guess worrying about Nationals made me a little crazy. I thought losing a couple of pounds would help me get more height in my jumps. So I cut back on what I've been eating. All I've had today is a yogurt and an apple."

Tori looked around for Veronica to back up her story again. But the spot where she and Evan had been sitting was empty. Veronica's purse and coat were gone. They must have moved fast, Tori thought. Veronica obviously didn't want Mrs. Carsen to see her with Evan.

"But you ate a big dinner last night," Tori's mother was pointing out.

"That's right," Natalia said. "We had spaghetti. You love spaghetti. And garlic bread. And a huge salad."

"I know, I know," Tori admitted. "And then I was worried that I ate way too much, so I cut back today to make up for it."

Mrs. Carsen looked doubtful. "I don't know, Tori. Something doesn't seem right to me. You've looked so pale, and you're always tired. . . . I think it's time to see Dr. Wyckoff, honey."

"I think that's a good idea," Kathy put in. "Just to be on the safe side."

"Please, Mom," Tori protested. "Come on. I'm okay. Just let me get something to eat and I promise I won't do this again, okay?"

Mrs. Carsen raised her eyebrows. "You won't get dizzy again?"

"I won't starve myself again," Tori snapped. "Please?" she said, changing her tone.

Mrs. Carsen shook her head. "Go get dressed," she said firmly. "Natalia, you go with her, in case she starts feeling dizzy again. I'm going to call Dr. Wyckoff and tell her we're coming. I'll get you a sandwich at the snack bar. You can eat it in the car." She pointed toward the locker room. "Now go."

Tori glared at her, but she stood up and slowly started toward the locker room. Natalia went with her.

Why did Kathy make Natalia call Mom? Tori thought. Now she would have to go to the doctor. She had a sick feeling in the pit of her stomach. She had managed to hide the way she felt from her mother so that she could keep skating. But she couldn't hide anything from Dr. Wyckoff. Her panic began to mount.

For weeks she'd been wondering if there was something terribly wrong with her.

She was finally going to find out.

10

"**D**id you call the doctor?" Tori asked a few minutes later.

She and her mother got into Mrs. Carsen's Jaguar.

"Yes," her mother answered. "She's meeting us at her office."

"Uh-huh," Tori said, but she wasn't really listening. She took a nibble from the tuna fish sandwich her mother had bought. But she wasn't hungry. She stuffed it back into its bag and set it on the dashboard.

Tori dreaded going to the doctor. She was sure Dr. Wyckoff would poke and prod and ask embarrassing questions. She was terrified of what the doctor might find wrong with her.

"You're not really hungry, are you?" Mrs. Carsen

said, breaking Tori's train of thought. "What's really wrong?"

Tori started to say, "Nothing." But then she realized that the lie was over. She didn't have to trick her mother or her friends anymore. She was going to the doctor whether she liked it or not. Good or bad, the truth would come out. Tori was still scared, but she also felt relieved. She was tired of being afraid of what might be wrong.

"I don't know—but something is wrong," she finally blurted out.

"How long have you thought something was wrong with you?" Mrs. Carsen demanded.

Tori looked down at her lap. "A month? Maybe more," she said quietly. "Ever since Sectionals."

Mrs. Carsen tightened her grip on the steering wheel. She eased the car onto Main Street.

"Why didn't you tell me sooner?" she finally asked. She sounded upset.

"I didn't want to have to stop practicing, Mom, that's all," Tori said. "I knew you wouldn't let me work on my long program if I told you I felt like something was wrong. And I knew you would drag me to the doctor."

Mrs. Carsen gave her a sidelong glance. "I would do whatever I thought was best for you," she said. "I worry about you because you're my child."

Tori reached down to rub the back of her calf. Ever since she'd left the ice the muscle in her right calf had felt tight. She'd never had a muscle cramp last as long as this one—not even over the past few weeks.

"Please tell me what's going on, honey," her mother pleaded.

All at once there was a lump in Tori's throat. She took a deep breath.

"I don't know. But I'm really worried, Mom," she blurted out.

"Why?" Mrs. Carsen asked. She took her eyes off the road long enough to search Tori's face. "Tell me, Tori."

"I didn't just get dizzy at the rink. I fainted. And I'm tired all the time, no matter how much I sleep. Sometimes I forget about it while I'm skating, and I can still skate fine. But other times it's a struggle just to do the simplest moves."

"That's stress, sweetheart," Mrs. Carsen said. "You get that from me. I get tired and achy when I work too hard on my business. You're worried about Nationals."

Tori shook her head. "My friends keep saying that, too. But . . ." She trailed off for a second. "The nurse at school thought I might have mono. She said I should get a blood test."

"The *nurse*?" Her mother looked startled. "When did you see her?"

"A little over a week ago," Tori said. "I fell asleep in the library, and the librarian sent me to the nurse."

"And you didn't tell me?" Mrs. Carsen demanded.

Tori looked down at her hands. "Nikki said her

cousin had to spend two weeks in bed when she had mono. I can't do that now! Besides, I don't feel that bad. But—"

Mrs. Carsen frowned. "But what?"

"But it's not just being tired," Tori confessed. "My muscles feel weak—even the ones in my feet."

"But Tori, you're bound to have sore muscles with the kind of workouts you do."

"It's different, Mom," Tori went on. "I can't really explain it. Today, right before practice, I was sitting at a table with a bottle of mineral water in my hand. All of a sudden, it fell on the table. It was as if all the strength just left my hand. It went totally weak on me."

"People drop things all the time, Tori. That doesn't mean anything."

Tori couldn't believe it. She had been holding in her fear for so long. Now she was finally telling her mother everything. And her mother was *under*reacting.

Tori was scared to admit that she was sick. But now she felt as if she had to talk her mother into believing it, too!

"This was different," Tori explained. "My hand muscles just collapsed on me. And my leg muscles have done that, too."

Mrs. Carsen was silent for a moment as they drove into the parking lot of the doctor's office.

"To me it sounds like stress, Tori," she said. "You are under very intense pressure." She turned the car engine off. "Whatever it is, I'm sure Dr. Wyckoff can help."

Tori didn't say anything. She looked at the two-story brick and glass medical building in front of them.

Her mother might be wrong about some things, like her opinion of Veronica. But she hoped her mother was right about this.

"Look straight ahead please, Tori," Dr. Wyckoff said.

She aimed a small light into Tori's right eye and peered into it. She used another light for Tori's ears. She listened to Tori's chest and back with a stethoscope. She dug her fingers into Tori's abdomen and asked her if it hurt. She had Tori walk a straight line across the room. She told her to close her eyes and touch her index fingers to her nose, one at a time. She tested the reflexes in Tori's legs by tapping just below her knee. And she asked questions about everything, from what Tori ate to what kinds of grades she got.

"All right," Dr. Wyckoff said finally. "You can get dressed now. Then come into my office, and we'll talk."

A few minutes later Dr. Wyckoff settled her slender frame behind a large oak desk.

"Well, the good news is that your physical exam was normal, Tori," she said. "I see no signs of infection in your lungs, ears, anywhere. Your blood pressure is normal. It's obvious you are in excellent physical condition from skating. Your muscle tone and standing pulse rate are excellent."

Tori and her mother exchanged smiles of relief.

"The bad news," Dr. Wyckoff continued, "is that I can't tell you what's wrong. I don't know why you're so tired, and I don't know why you fainted this afternoon. I'm concerned about this tightness in your muscles and the sudden weakness in your hands and legs."

"But—" Tori interrupted. Dr. Wyckoff silenced her by putting one hand up as if she were a traffic cop.

"So we're not through with you yet," she said. "First, we need to do some blood work." She wrote something on a pad and handed it to Tori's mother. "Unfortunately, the lab is closed today. You'll have to go there on Monday, and then it will take a week to ten days to get the results. I also want Tori to see a colleague of mine—Edith Barnard. She's a muscle specialist."

The doctor picked up a pen and tapped it on the desk. "I want to emphasize that these tests are very routine. We'll be looking at lots of different things, just ruling out some of the more obvious possibilities."

Mrs. Carsen's eyebrows lifted and she sat up straight.

"Possibilities?" she said. "What are you talking about?"

Tori looked anxiously from her mother to the doctor.

Dr. Wyckoff ticked names off on her fingers. "Mononucleosis, Epstein-Barr virus, Lyme disease, connective-tissue diseases. . . ." She stopped. "Those are just some of the possibilities."

Tori's eyes widened, and she gripped the arms of her chair.

"Those sound bad," she said. "Really bad."

"Don't let it scare you, Tori," Dr. Wyckoff said. "I don't see any evidence from your physical exam of any of these diseases. And let me add that serious disease is quite rare in someone of your age and physical condition. But we do have to rule them out. So let's get the blood tests done and let's have Dr. Barnard take a look at you and we'll see what we see. Until then, all we really know is that your physical exam is normal."

"I don't understand," Tori said. "Am I sick or not?"

Dr. Wyckoff rubbed her finger along the edge of Tori's file.

"Let's put it this way. You could be suffering from stress. Or maybe you're tired a lot because you're growing fast. Or maybe the blood tests will show us something. Whatever it is, we'll find it."

"What about skating?" Tori asked. "I can still skate, can't I? I'm going to Nationals in two weeks. I *have* to practice."

"I see no reason why you shouldn't continue your normal routine. Take it easy, though. Rest a lot. Don't push yourself too hard."

"We'll make sure of that," Mrs. Carsen said, smiling. She looked at Tori. "With your skating ability and the new routine, you don't need to practice as much anyway."

Tori stared back at her mother, dumbstruck. My skating ability? My new routine? she thought. My skating ability is almost zero. And I can't even *do* my new routine. Is this the mother who used to come to all my practices? The mother who used to know *everything* about me?

"I knew it was just stress, sweetheart," Mrs. Carsen told Tori. She patted her arm briskly.

"We can't be sure of that just yet, Mrs. Carsen," Dr. Wyckoff said. "But for now there is nothing to indicate to me that Tori's condition would be worsened by skating."

The doctor looked straight at Tori.

"Just continue with your normal activities for now. And for you, skating is normal. If I find out anything that leads me to believe skating could be harmful, you'll be the first to know."

"What about competing?" Mrs. Carsen asked. "That's very rigorous. That's why Tori is so stressed now."

Dr. Wyckoff tapped the pen on the table, considering. "This competition is when?"

"We're leaving in two weeks," Tori said, leaning forward.

"In that case, I think we can hold off on making a decision for a while. Let's talk after I get the results of the blood tests," Dr. Wyckoff concluded.

Walking out to the car a few minutes later, both Tori and her mother were silent for a minute.

"How do you feel now?" her mother said as she unlocked the doors of the Jaguar.

"Truthfully, Mom?" Tori said. "Confused."

Her mother gave Tori a puzzled look.

"I mean, I thought there was something really, really wrong with me," Tori said. "So I'm kind of relieved that it might be stress. On the other hand, I can't believe I just have *stress*. I've been in a lot of big competitions before. And I never felt like this. Never."

Mrs. Carsen turned the Jaguar onto the road.

"Nationals isn't just any competition, Tori," she said. "This is the biggest competition of your life."

Tori sank lower into her seat. She had a sudden thought that scared her. Her mother didn't want to believe anything could be wrong!

"Even if it is just stress, it's ruining my skating," Tori finally said. "My body doesn't even feel like it's mine anymore!"

"We'll talk to Dan," her mother answered. "Coaches know all about stress."

Tori sighed. Dan would know what to tell her about

stress. She would listen carefully and do everything he said. Whatever was blocking her skating had to be fixed.

One thing was for sure, she realized. If she was going to stand a chance at Nationals, she couldn't take Dr. Wyckoff's advice. Taking it easy was the last thing she could do.

11

Later that night, Tori rolled over on her bed and let her copy of *Jane Eyre* drop to the floor. There's no point in even trying to do homework, she decided. No matter how hard she tried to concentrate on the page in front of her, her thoughts kept going back to her visit to the doctor.

She wished she could have the blood tests and get the results right away. She wouldn't get answers until right before Nationals.

There was a quiet knock at the door.

"Come in," Tori called, sitting up. Veronica slipped in, closing the door behind her.

"Hi," Tori said without enthusiasm.

"Hi." Veronica pulled out Tori's desk chair and sat down. Tori noticed that she'd changed out of the clothes she'd worn earlier. Now she had on a brown-

and-beige miniskirt with a matching cotton-knit sweater that zipped up the front.

"Don't you ever wear the same outfit for a whole day?" Tori asked.

Veronica ignored the question. "So what did the doctor say?" she asked. "Did she know what was wrong with you?"

"They're going to do some tests on Monday," Tori answered. "Mom thinks it's just stress."

"Oh," Veronica said. She picked a little piece of lint off her skirt. "Do *you* think it's stress?"

Tori looked at Veronica. She was about to say, "Of course." That's what she had said to Haley, and Nikki, and everyone else who had called her this afternoon. But suddenly she found herself blurting out something else.

"I don't know! I feel so bad. How can stress do that? I've had stress before. Crazy megastress. And it made me skate *better*. Now I have days when I can't even finish my routine. I've been skating my whole life so I could make Nationals. And I'm afraid I'm going to blow it."

She stood up and started pacing back and forth.

She stopped in front of her bookshelves. Her old, stuffed elephant—Elly Nells—stared back. She remembered when she never slept without Elly Nells. She grabbed the animal and held it.

"If you blow Nationals, does that mean you won't make it to the Olympics, either?" Veronica asked.

Tori nodded, afraid even to think that far ahead.

"See—that *is* more stress," Veronica said. "And now that you know it's probably stress, you can deal. Didn't you say your New Age coach is great at that stuff?"

Tori sighed. Why was everyone so sure she was stressed out?

She changed the subject. "Thanks for sticking up for me at the rink today with Kathy."

Veronica shrugged. "No problem," she said. "I guess it didn't work, though, did it?"

"Guess not," Tori said.

"Did your mother say anything about seeing me with Evan at the rink?" Veronica asked, looking worried.

Tori smiled and shook her head. "No. You guys took off so fast, she didn't have a chance to spot you."

"Good," Veronica said.

"But you'd better be careful, Veronica," Tori warned her. "Mom will have a fit if she finds out you're dating a guy who's in college. And something tells me that Roger wouldn't like it much, either."

"So? Tell me something I don't already know," Veronica said.

"Aren't you worried?" Tori asked.

"Not really." Veronica shrugged. "I'll do whatever I have to to make sure they don't find out. Besides, he's worth it," she added, smiling happily.

"He does seem like a nice guy," Tori said.

"Evan is the sweetest guy I ever met. And he's smart, too," Veronica informed her.

"Then why is he dating someone who just turned sixteen years old?" Tori couldn't resist asking.

Veronica's smile faded. "Actually, he thinks I'm eighteen," she mumbled.

"*What?*" Tori screeched. "You lied to him, too?"

"Sort of," Veronica said, smoothing back her hair. "I met him at the library over at the junior college. Betsy and I go there all the time, you know."

"To study?" Tori said doubtfully.

Veronica grinned. "Actually, it's a great place to meet guys," she said.

Tori just shook her head.

"Anyway, Betsy talked to Evan first, and she told him we were seniors in high school."

"And he believed you?" Tori asked.

"Sure." Veronica shrugged again. "I don't like lying all the time, but I never really expected to like Evan this much." She paused for a second. "I've thought about telling him the truth. But if I do, he'll break up with me. He thinks people should go out with people their own age when they first start dating. You wouldn't guess it from looking at him, but Evan is . . . he's *really* straight."

Tori was surprised to see that Veronica looked upset.

"Why are you so worried about lying to Evan?" she asked. "Cutting school and forging signatures isn't exactly honest, and you do those things all the time."

"I know, but that's different," Veronica said impatiently. "What I meant was, I don't want to lie to someone I like as much as I like Evan."

Tori felt a twinge of sympathy for Veronica. "What are you going to do?" she asked.

Veronica smiled. "Cross my fingers and hope for the best," she said. "What else *can* I do?"

"Nothing, I guess," Tori replied. She grinned, too. "In the meantime, you'd better be nice to me. I could tell Evan or my mom the truth at any time, you know."

"You could," Veronica said as she stood up. "But I know you won't," she added, reaching for the door-knob. "I'll see you later."

As Veronica left the room, Tori lay down on her bed again and tucked Elly Nells under her chin. "Can you believe that was Veronica who just left the room?" she said to the stuffed elephant.

Tori was amazed by the conversation she'd just had with Veronica. So much had changed, she realized with a start. Just two weeks before, Tori had been dying to tell her mother about Evan and Veronica, but now she felt very different. Evan was much nicer than she'd first thought. Veronica could be nice too.

What surprised Tori most was how honest she had been with Veronica. She hadn't even told Haley, her very best friend, how scared she felt. Instead, she had shared her fears with Veronica.

Veronica!

Who would have believed it?

❤ ❤

Tori spent Monday morning in Dr. Barnard's office getting poked, prodded, and stuck with needles until she wanted to scream. That afternoon she went to the lab with her mother. One technician drew blood, and another took several X rays. The man who did the X rays told Tori's mother that it would take about ten days to get the results.

That's right before Nationals, Tori thought, trying not to panic.

As they headed out to the parking lot, Tori's mother reached out and held her hand.

"Don't worry, honey," she said. "You can still go to skating practice. Just don't overdo anything. Your health is a lot more important than winning a gold medal at Nationals. You'll just have to settle for a silver or a bronze this time around." She pinched Tori's cheek playfully. "Okay, sweetie?"

Tori just nodded, without bothering to reply.

"In the meantime," Mrs. Carsen went on, "you'll eat well and get plenty of rest. And I . . ."

As they got into the car, Tori leaned over and pushed the Play button on the CD player. She wanted to tune out her mother. Classical guitar music filled the car, and her mother's voice faded. Tori closed her eyes. She concentrated on the music and breathed deeply.

Just relax, she told herself. Because if you keep getting stressed and then skating the way you have been, you'll *really* have something to worry about at Nationals!

12

"**O**kay, Tori! That's enough for today," Dan Trapp called out. "Can I have a word with you before you go?"

He waved Tori over to where he was standing at the boards.

It was the day after Tori had gone to the specialist and the lab. Tori knew her mother had called Dan at home that night and filled him in.

Tori glided up to Dan and leaned on the rail. She tried to catch her breath. Dan gave her a worried look.

"That second triple-triple isn't going too well," he said quietly. "I think you have enough on your hands with the first triple-triple. You have some other very hard elements in your program. It will be enough."

Tori stood up straight and stared at Dan.

"Are you saying we should take out the second tri-ple-triple jump?" she asked.

"Exactly," Dan said. "With the way you've been skating lately, it seems to be too much for you, Tori. You know that, and I know that."

Tori turned away from Dan and swiped at a tear that threatened to roll down her cheek. She turned back to him.

"I do know," she said, trying not to sob. "But hav-ing two triple-triple jumps was going to make my pro-gram stand out."

"Your program will still stand out, Tori," Dan said, putting his hand on her arm. "You are a great skater. Even without the second triple-triple, you will still stand out."

"Stand out. Ha!" Tori laughed bitterly. "My pro-gram is going to stand out because I won't be able to finish it. Even *without* the second triple-triple combi-nation."

"Hey!" Dan said gently. "Is this the Tori I know?"

Tori was silent for a minute.

"No, Dan," she said, choking back more tears. "It's *not* the Tori you know. *That* Tori skated her program perfectly a few weeks ago. Remember? I don't know who *this* Tori is."

"Calm down," Dan said. "You're just making your-self feel worse."

"Worse?" Tori said. "How could I feel worse?"

Dan shook his head. "I'm sorry, Tori. Really sorry."

Tori walked off the ice. She picked up her guards and slipped them onto her skates.

"I'll see you, Dan," she said, and headed toward the locker room.

The next ten days passed in a horrible blur. Tori got up every morning and went to skating practice, and to school, and back to skating practice. She did her best not to think about how tired she felt.

She had been taking vitamins, doing yoga, drinking health shakes, and practicing breathing exercises. Dan had cut her practices down by ten minutes each. That and getting some extra sleep had helped a little.

But Tori felt desperate. Even without the second triple-triple jump combination, she was having trouble. By the time she got to the end of her routine on most days, her legs felt heavy and tired and she was breathing way too hard. Her skating looked wooden and unnatural. She was struggling to get through each move, and it showed.

It was Thursday, and her blood-test results hadn't come back yet. She was leaving for Nationals the next day.

"Where's Mom?" Tori asked as she, Roger, and Natalia walked into the kitchen after practice. She and Natalia tossed their Silver Blades jackets over a chair. "How come you picked us up instead?"

Roger didn't answer.

"Is Mom shopping or something?" Tori asked.

Roger shook his head. "She, um, she had some work to get done at the office before we drop Nat off at the train station and then leave for Philadelphia tomorrow."

"Oh," Tori replied, surprised. She'd expected her mother to be at home, overseeing the packing and making sure Tori's skating dresses were ready.

She would be wearing a maroon velvet dress for her long program. Her mother had designed it without getting Tori's opinion. Mrs. Carsen wanted it to be a surprise. And it had been.

The surprise was that Tori hated the dress. She didn't like the way the red fabric looked against her skin. And the velvet material made her waist look thick.

Tori had always *loved* the skating dresses her mother designed for her. Now it seemed as if she and her mother were so far out of touch that her mother didn't even know her taste anymore.

Her mother had looked very anxious when she held the dress out and asked Tori if she liked it.

Tori decided on the spot that she had told so many lies to her mother, she could tell one more. One that might do some good.

"I love it, Mom," she had said. Her mother had looked so relieved!

What does it matter if the dress looks dumb, anyway? Tori thought now. She was going to skate so badly at Nationals, she might as well look bad, too.

With a sigh, Tori realized that she had been thinking negative thoughts for the past two weeks. She had lost every ounce of her confidence—the confidence that used to make her soar when she skated.

Roger's voice broke into her thoughts.

"Actually, that's why she asked me to pick you and Natalia up," he was saying. He began unloading the bag of take-out food they'd picked up on the way home. "Her business is doing so well, it's getting harder and harder for her to take time off."

I noticed, Tori thought. Her mother had only come to about half of Tori's practices. And she hadn't said anything about the way Tori was skating.

Tori covered her mouth with her hand as she yawned. She'd worked harder today than she had all week, and she was exhausted. She bent down to massage her legs as the familiar cramps started in her feet and ran up into her calves.

"Tori?"

She looked up. Roger was watching her closely.

"You look pretty tired," he said. "Was practice too much for you today?"

"No. I'm fine," Tori said. "Really."

Natalia smiled. "You should have seen her nail her triple toe loop–triple toe loop, Roger. She looked like a medal winner to me!"

"That's great." Roger smiled as he started taking

lids off the cartons of food. "Well, Dr. Wyckoff told your mother that she consulted with Dr. Barnard. And she said the results from your lab tests should be in today or tomorrow. She's not sure why it took this long."

"Whatever," Tori said casually. She quickly turned her back on Roger and Natalia and started making a cup of tea so that they wouldn't see her worried expression.

A few minutes later, Roger went upstairs to change his clothes and start packing for the next day's trip. As Tori sat down at the table with Natalia to drink her tea, Mrs. Carsen walked in through the back door.

"Hi, Mom," Tori greeted her.

"Hello," Natalia chimed in.

"Hi, girls," Mrs. Carsen said. She set her briefcase on the kitchen counter, and Tori noticed that her hand was shaking. The lines on her face seemed somehow deeper, too, as if she had gotten older since that morning.

Mrs. Carsen walked to the bottom of the stairs and called Roger. Something in her voice made Tori's heart beat a little faster.

Oh no, Tori thought. What's wrong? She sat on the stool at the kitchen counter, afraid to move or even breathe.

Her mother came back into the kitchen, and Roger followed right behind her. "Is Veronica here?" Mrs. Carsen asked.

Roger shook his head. "She's out with Betsy," he said.

Mrs. Carsen nodded, then drew in a deep breath. "I wanted you all to hear this," she said. "But we can fill in Veronica later, when she gets home."

Tori swallowed hard. "Hear what, Mom?" she managed to ask.

Her mother didn't look at Tori. "We, uh, might have to change our plans to go to Philadelphia tomorrow."

"What?" Tori felt all the color drain out of her face. She was glad that she was sitting because she didn't think her legs would hold her. She knew it! She knew there was something wrong.

"Why?" Natalia asked, looking confused.

Mrs. Carsen's face had turned pale, too. Tori watched her mother grab the back of the kitchen chair, as if to steady herself.

"Dr. Wyckoff called me a few minutes ago," Tori's mother said. "She finally got back the test results."

The kitchen was completely silent as they all waited for Mrs. Carsen to go on. Tori gripped the spoon that she'd used to stir her cup of tea.

"She didn't tell me the results. But Dr. Wyckoff wants us to come in tomorrow morning before we leave for Philadelphia," Mrs. Carsen said. "She didn't want to discuss it over the phone. But she said it was very important."

Just then her eyes met Roger's. The worried glance that passed between them made Tori's breath catch in her throat.

"It's not good news, is it, Mom?" Tori said. Her voice sounded odd, even to herself.

"I don't know, honey," Mrs. Carsen said. Her voice was shaking. "But let's not get too worried. We'll see what the doctor says tomorrow."

Tori felt her right hand go weak, and the spoon in her fingers made a loud clatter as it dropped onto the table. Slowly she raised her frightened eyes to her mother's.

"What's wrong with me?" she whispered.

13

Inside the waiting room at Dr. Wyckoff's office the next morning, Tori stared at the clock—8:03, 8:04. She and her family had arrived a few minutes ago, but she felt as if they'd been waiting for hours.

As the minutes ticked by, Tori's hands felt clammy, and her stomach did flip-flops. All she could think about was what Dr. Wyckoff would say. Would the doctor say Tori was okay, and that she just didn't give test results over the phone? Or would she tell Tori she was really sick? Maybe Tori had mono and the doctor was going to say she couldn't skate at Nationals.

Finally the door of the inside offices opened, and a nurse poked her head out. "Tori Carsen?"

Tori swallowed hard. Then she stood up on shaky legs. "That's me."

Her mother and Roger stood up, followed by Natalia and Veronica.

Tori scowled at her mother. "The whole family's coming with me?" she whispered sharply.

Mrs. Carsen shifted her purse to the other shoulder. "I think it's a good idea, Tori," she said uneasily. "We all want to help you."

"I'm not a baby!" Tori snapped.

Then she looked at Natalia's and Veronica's hurt expressions.

"I'm sorry, you guys," she said. "I guess I'm nervous and I'm taking it out on you."

The girls nodded at Tori.

"We understand," Natalia said.

Tori and her family walked over to the door and down the corridor behind the nurse.

"Please go in and sit down." The nurse gestured at Dr. Wyckoff's private office at the end of the hall. "The doctor will be with you in a minute."

As she stepped into the room, Tori's hands turned ice cold. The few minutes they'd spent in the waiting room had passed so slowly. Now it felt as if time were speeding by. It was all Tori could do to stay in the office. She wanted to turn around and bolt out the door.

Roger and Mrs. Carsen sat on the couch while Natalia and Veronica took chairs. Veronica had brought a fashion magazine in from the waiting room. For the next few minutes, the only sound in the room was the snap of pages as she flipped through them at a furious pace.

Tori was too nervous to sit still. She stayed on her feet, walking all around Dr. Wyckoff's office, pretending to be interested in the things scattered around the room. It was paneled in dark wood and had soft lighting. Several diplomas hung on the walls.

As she walked around the doctor's cluttered desk, she saw a small pewter frame sitting on top of a stack of papers. Curious, she picked up the frame and looked at the photo inside. It was a snapshot of two grinning little boys standing together on the beach. They must be Dr. Wyckoff's sons, Tori thought.

The boys looked as if they didn't have a care in the world. Tears unexpectedly sprang to Tori's eyes. She couldn't remember the last time she had felt that carefree. She could barely remember what it felt like to live without a deep pit of fear in her stomach.

Just then the door opened, and Dr. Wyckoff stepped into the room.

"Good morning, folks," she said briskly. Tori quickly replaced the photo, and the doctor pointed to an empty leather chair. "Why don't you sit, Tori?"

Tori nodded, feeling her whole body tremble as she walked over and sat in the chair.

Dr. Wyckoff tucked a strand of her dark hair behind her ear. "I'm afraid the news I have is not good," she began.

Tori froze. In the armchair beside her, she saw Veronica look up from her magazine.

"We think that Tori has a very rare disease called myotonic muscular dystrophy," Dr. Wyckoff went on.

"What?" Tori's mother gasped. "I've never heard of that before."

Tori could hear the panic in her mother's voice. Roger leaned over and placed a hand on her arm.

"It's a rare hereditary disease," Dr. Wyckoff explained. "It affects the muscles, mostly the muscles of the hands, arms, and feet. Patients often have problems with their eyes, too."

"But my eyes are fine," Tori blurted out. "So is the rest of me, most of the time."

Dr. Wyckoff nodded. "In your case, the disease seems to be affecting your hands, causing weakness. Another thing you might have noticed is that you have trouble letting go of things."

Tori nodded, but she couldn't speak.

Dr. Wyckoff went on talking about myotonic dystrophy, but Tori stopped listening.

I have myotonic muscular dystrophy? she thought in disbelief. I have a serious disease? This can't be happening!

Mrs. Carsen sat rigid, her face white, as Dr. Wyckoff continued talking.

Then, dimly, Tori heard Roger ask another question. "How will this affect Tori over time?"

Dr. Wyckoff sighed. "I'm sorry to say that what we know about myotonic dystrophy is not great news. The progression of the disease is that the muscles lose their strength and gradually waste away."

Mrs. Carsen gasped.

"Does that mean Tori's going to get worse?" Roger asked.

"I'm sorry to say that the answer is most likely yes," Dr. Wyckoff answered. "We don't usually see signs of this disease until someone's in their early twenties. Some people with it have no symptoms until fairly late in life. But when it starts this early . . . we take it more seriously."

The doctor said the last words very quietly, almost as if she didn't want Tori to hear them.

Tori blinked. "Does that mean I could *die* from this?" she asked.

Dr. Wyckoff shook her head quickly. "No, Tori. People with this type of dystrophy generally have normal life spans."

The doctor opened a drawer in her desk and pulled out a pamphlet. She handed it to Tori.

"This will answer some of your questions before we meet again," she told Tori. "Later we can talk about . . . about some of the, um, limitations myotonic dystrophy might cause in your life."

"Limitations?" Mrs. Carsen finally spoke up. "What are you talking about, Dr. Wyckoff?"

"We have to face the possibility that Tori could lose most of the use of her legs," Dr. Wyckoff said. "At some point, she will probably require a wheelchair."

Wheelchair?

Oh, no! No! No! No! Tori thought. A wheelchair? *Me* in a wheelchair?

Tori gripped the chair's leather armrests as she began to feel her world slip away. It's over, a voice said
inside her head. Your whole life—shopping at the
mall, going to school, hanging out with your friends.
You're never going to do those things again.

Somehow the worst part didn't sink in for several
minutes. But when the thought finally hit her, it made
her gasp for breath.

I can't skate anymore.

Tears streamed down Tori's face. Her whole life was
skating. For seven years, ever since she'd joined Silver
Blades, all she'd thought about and dreamed about
was going to Nationals and the Olympics. But
now . . .

Silent sobs racked Tori's body.

Across the room, her mother had buried her face in
her hands.

"But . . ." Veronica looked up at Dr. Wyckoff. "But
we're on our way to Philadelphia," she went on.
"Tori's supposed to compete in Nationals next week.
Can she still skate?"

Tori looked up, waiting to hear Dr. Wyckoff's answer. The doctor handed several tissues to Tori, then
gave the box to Mrs. Carsen. When she finally answered Veronica's question, she looked directly at Tori.

"That's a decision only you can make, Tori," she
said quietly. "At this point, we don't know how fast the
disease is going to progress. Skating is very rigorous.
You might find it difficult to skate with the same energy you once had.

"However," the doctor went on, still speaking to Tori, "maybe the exercise will help you retain some muscle strength."

Dr. Wyckoff sighed.

"I'd like you to see Dr. Barnard again—the specialist you went to before," she said. "She can tell you more."

Mrs. Carsen glared at the doctor.

"A specialist," she repeated coolly. "I think a specialist is *exactly* what we need to see. But we'll find our own this time."

Mrs. Carsen turned toward Natalia, Veronica, and Tori.

"Why don't you girls wait outside," she said sharply. "Roger and I have a few more questions for the doctor."

Tori numbly followed Natalia and Veronica back to the waiting room, feeling as if she were dreaming.

Suddenly she heard her mother's voice drifting down the hall.

"We'll see our own specialist," Mrs. Carsen was shouting. "You and that Dr. Barnard can't even diagnose an illness properly! It's ridiculous to even think that Tori has myo—, mya—"

The doctor murmured something that Tori couldn't hear.

"I don't care *who* Dr. Barnard is!" Mrs. Carsen shouted. "She obviously doesn't know what she's doing!"

The doctor murmured again, and Tori heard her mother shout back.

"No, *you* calm down, Doctor," Mrs. Carsen shrieked.

This can't be happening, Tori thought numbly. This can't be me that Dr. Wyckoff and Mom are arguing about.

But deep down Tori wasn't surprised. She'd known for weeks that something was wrong with her body. She had hoped that if she ignored it, and never talked about it, the disease would go away.

But it didn't go away, Tori thought. And now it has a name—myotonic dystrophy.

14

As Tori sat with Natalia and Veronica in the waiting room, Natalia reached over and squeezed Tori's hand sympathetically.

"I wish I weren't catching the next train to go stay with my father. Maybe I should stay here now, since I guess you're not going to Philadelphia after all," Natalia said. Her eyes brimmed with tears. "I'm so very sorry, Tori. All your dreams and your hopes—"

"Oh, please, Natalia," Veronica cut in impatiently. "I know you're upset, but you don't have to go on and on like that."

Tori blinked in surprise. She couldn't believe how heartless Veronica sounded. She must have been crazy to think that she and Veronica were getting along better lately.

As Tori turned to face Veronica, she could feel all her shock and worry and fear boil up into a fury.

"I know you don't think much of my skating," Tori snapped at Veronica. The coldness in her voice surprised even Tori. "But don't you care just a little bit that I'm not going to Nationals?"

Veronica adjusted the hem of her miniskirt. "Who said you're *not* going to Nationals?" she said calmly.

"Dr. Wyckoff!" Tori shot back. "Maybe you were too busy looking at clothes in that stupid magazine to hear what she said. But for your information, I have a rare disease and I'm probably going to spend the rest of my life in a wheelchair!"

Veronica's expression didn't change. "Actually, that's not what I heard," she said evenly. "I was listening quite carefully and I heard Dr. Wyckoff say that you *could* skate, Tori."

Tori gestured angrily at the door that led to the interior offices. "Do you honestly think my mother is going to let me take a risk like that?"

Natalia spoke up. "But Dr. Wyckoff said skating is *your* decision, Tori," she said.

"*Exactly,*" Veronica said. "I know your mom likes to control things, especially when it comes to your skating, but it's your life, Tori—even if you are only fifteen." She reached into her bag for a tube of lipstick and deftly applied it to her lips. "I know what I'd do if I were you," she said a moment later. "I'd go for it."

"And take the chance that you'd fall or make a fool of yourself?" Tori demanded.

"Yup." Veronica's tone softened. "Look, Tori. You don't know how much longer you're going to be able to use your legs. If I were you, I'd want to skate for as long as I could. And I especially wouldn't want to miss the chance to go to Nationals."

Before Tori could reply, her mother burst through the door to the waiting room. Roger was right on her heels. Mrs. Carsen had stopped crying, but her eyes were still rimmed with red, and her face looked pale.

"Oh, my poor baby," she murmured, sweeping Tori into her arms and hugging her tight. "My poor, poor little girl."

Her mother released her, and Roger hugged Tori, too.

"Come on, let's go home," Mrs. Carsen said. "I'm going to call our own specialist so we can get to the bottom of this. With luck, they'll be able to fit you in today or tomorrow."

"But . . . But Nationals, Mom," Tori stammered. "What about our trip to Philadelphia?"

Mrs. Carsen shook her head firmly. "I'm sorry, honey, but you'll have to forget about Nationals. I'm not letting you skate anymore until we know exactly what's wrong with you."

"But . . . ," Tori protested. "But we *do* know what's wrong. The doctor just said I—"

"Come on, girls," Mrs. Carsen said, cutting Tori off. She pulled her purse over her shoulder. "I would like to get home and start making some calls."

While her mother walked to the coat rack, Tori stood up slowly.

"It's your life," Veronica whispered in her ear as she brushed past Tori to get her jacket.

Tori stood there, still not moving. Veronica's right, she thought. It *is* my life.

Tori had dreaded going to Nationals. But now the idea of not going made her feel worse. Competing there was her lifelong dream. And she was going through with it. Even if she skated badly, she would know she had tried.

"Here's your coat, Tori," Mrs. Carsen said, holding out the brown suede jacket.

As Tori took it, she drew in a breath. "I'm not going home, Mom," she said softly.

"*What?*" Mrs. Carsen wheeled around, panic in her blue eyes.

"I'm not going home," Tori repeated. She cleared her throat. "I want to skate in Nationals."

"Now, Tori," Roger said in a warning tone. "You haven't had time to think this through."

"Yes I have," Tori started. "And I—"

"This isn't your decision, Tori," Mrs. Carsen interrupted sharply. A spark of anger flared in her eyes. "You're fifteen years old. You're not capable of making the right choices for yourself right now."

Tori swallowed and stood up straight. It was true that she had made a lot of *bad* choices lately. She had been sneaking around and lying—and then making excuses for her behavior. But she wouldn't do it anymore. She would never do it again.

She knew that her decision to go to Nationals, even though she was terrified, was the best and bravest decision she had made in months.

"It is the right choice, Mom. I have to go," she said. As she spoke, she felt herself growing more sure. "And Dr. Wyckoff seemed to think that going to Nationals is my decision."

"Well, you're not Dr. Wyckoff's daughter," her mother shot back. "You're *my* daughter, and I . . ." Without warning, Mrs. Carsen's face crumpled and she burst into tears.

"Oh, Mom," Tori murmured. She felt a lump rise in her throat as her mother sobbed loudly.

"I'm sorry, Tori," Mrs. Carsen choked out. "I'm trying to be strong, but I love you so much, and you've worked so hard on your skating and . . ."

"Then let me go, Mom," Tori pleaded softly. "I want to skate in Nationals more than anything. And you heard Dr. Wyckoff—this might be my only chance."

There was a long silence as her mother hugged Tori tightly. Finally Mrs. Carsen pulled away. She reached out to lift Tori's chin so that Tori had to look her right in the eye.

"Okay, we'll go," she relented. "But on one condition."

"What?" Tori asked.

"I'm going to get the name of another specialist,

one we can consult while we're in Philadelphia," her mother said briskly. "The second we reach the city, you'll go in for an appointment."

"Okay, Mom," Tori promised. "Anything."

"Well, then, let's get going," Roger said.

Tori put on her coat and followed her family into the hall.

When Mrs. Carsen and Roger weren't looking, Veronica flashed Tori a thumbs-up. "You know something?" she whispered. "I think I'm a good influence on you."

Tori shook her head and burst out laughing.

But as they walked to the parking lot, Tori realized that it was true. Veronica *had* been a good influence on her. If it hadn't been for Veronica, Tori might not have found the strength—and the courage—to stick up for herself.

She hoped the specialist would tell her there was nothing wrong. That Dr. Wyckoff or Dr. Barnard or the lab had made a big mistake. That all Tori had was a case of mononucleosis.

Tori couldn't believe that a few weeks ago she had been scared of mono! Now she wished that was all she had. As she climbed into Roger's Mercedes, she made another grown-up decision.

I'm not going to worry about the future, she decided. I'm going to focus on the present. Because that's all I have right now.

As Roger started up the engine and drove away from the medical building, a small ripple of excitement went through Tori. They would drop Natalia at the train station and then get onto the highway. In a few hours, they would be in Philadelphia for the most important figure-skating competition in the United States.

Tori didn't know if she would be able to skate at Nationals next year. She didn't even know if she would be able to skate at all by then. So she was going to go to Philadelphia and skate as she had never skated before.

And she was going to skate as if she would never skate *again*.

Tori was going to skate as if her life depended on it.

TO BE CONTINUED . . .

Don't miss Now or Never, *Book Two in the Gold Medal Dreams three-book miniseries!*

NOW OR NEVER

Tori's dream of skating for the national title turns into a nightmare when she learns that she has a terrible muscle disease. It might put her in a wheelchair for the rest of her life.

Tori's mother doesn't want her to compete at Nationals. The stress could make Tori even sicker. But that's a chance Tori plans to take.

If she wants to make her dream come true, Tori has to skate now . . .

Or never.

Turn the page to read an exciting chapter from Now or Never, *on sale at your local bookstore next month!*

6

"This is it, Tori," Dan Trapp said. "One-third of your score."

It was Wednesday morning, the day of the short program. Tori stood near the opening in the boards. Dan was squeezing a knot out of one of her shoulders. He was giving her a pep talk at the same time.

"Lucky for us, Cara Hopkins isn't here because of her sprained ankle. She would have given you some major competition.

"But you're still up against some of the biggest skaters," Dan continued. "Amber, Jill, Carla. You know they're good. You've also got to beat Tracy Wilkins and Fiona Bartlet.

"Still, I've seen you skate better than all of them," Dan concluded. "If you concentrate and give it your all, you'll easily finish in the top three."

Tori nodded. She was listening to Dan. But she also kept thinking about what results would come from the latest batch of medical tests. Tori forced herself to concentrate only on what Dan was saying.

"Go warm up. Don't use too much energy practicing your jumps. Nail them and quit," Dan said. He gave her a light push toward the ice.

Tori was in the final group of skaters warming up on the ice. Jill and Carla were there too. Jill wore a soft pink chiffon dress with flowing cap sleeves and a laced bodice. Carla was in a tight white dress with purple feathers. Tori smoothed her blue satin dress and fluffed out the short, lacy skirt.

She skated around the rink, trying to get her muscles warm. It took several trips. Soon she was stroking smoothly and powerfully. She felt a surge of hope. Maybe she'd skate her short program well, even though she felt rotten. When the five-minute warm-up ended, Tori skated off the ice.

Dan Trapp took her aside and held both of her hands.

"Go find a private place to focus," he ordered. "Relax, and picture your short program in your mind. See yourself skating every move perfectly. Okay?"

Tori nodded.

"I'll see you right before you step on the ice," Dan said.

Tori walked to the cavernous backstage area of the arena. She found a quiet corner and dragged over a metal folding chair. She plunked down and took a deep breath. She pictured her routine. She saw herself moving through the spins and jumps to her music.

Tori felt a nervous hum in her stomach. She was slightly queasy, but excited too. It was a familiar feeling. She got it before every competition.

Tori tried not to dwell on how important the short program was. But she couldn't block out her nervous thoughts. The short program called for her to complete several required elements, including a double axel and lots of fancy footwork. Would she be strong enough for the jump? Would her muscles be loose enough for her to make her footwork look graceful and coordinated? Tori felt her stomach cramp up in knots.

Mrs. Carsen walked in and sat next to Tori. She smoothed Tori's hair with her long, cool fingers. "Relax, Tori," she said.

Tori folded her arms and took several deep breaths. She never watched the skaters who went ahead of her. It was too nerve-racking. But the sounds of the first skater's music filtered into the room.

Tori recognized it as Carla's piece. She knew that Carla's flashy style would show in everything she did. All her moves had a flourish, and she always shot confident smiles at the judges. She was like a cheerleader.

Next came Jill's music. Tori had seen Jill's newest short program. If Tori hadn't been so nervous, she would have loved seeing it again. Jill's long legs and quiet confidence made her skating look like a ballet solo. Everything she did looked easy—even her triple Lutz–double toe loop.

Dan appeared at the entrance of the backstage area. He pointed to his watch.

"It's time, Tori," he called.

Tori sighed and stood up. Her mother stood too.

"I'll be watching with Dan," Mrs. Carsen said. "Good luck, sweetheart."

Tori walked over to Dan. Her coach put his arm around her as they made their way to the rink.

"Take it easy, Tori," Dan said. "Have some fun out there. I've seen you do this program beautifully a hundred times. Today doesn't have to be different."

As Tori and Dan walked closer to the rink, her old confidence came back. The cool air of the rink, the heaviness of her skates, even the butterflies in her stomach—it all felt familiar. This was her life. Skating was all she knew, and she loved it.

Tori took a deep breath and peered around the arena. Crowds of people packed the bleachers, chattering and rustling their programs. Television cameras pointed at the well-lit ice.

"Tori!" a reporter called. "Over here!"

Dan waved the reporter off. Tori ducked her head and kept walking toward the opening in the boards. She pulled off her skate guards and handed them to Dan.

"Good luck," he said. He squeezed Tori's hand. "Knock 'em dead."

Tori put the television cameras and judges out of her mind. It was time to focus. The announcer called her name. Tori skated to center ice to the sound of applause. She thought she could hear Natalia shouting, "Go, Tori!"

Tori struck her opening pose. The strains of Jacques Offenbach's "Gaité Parisienne" began. Tori loved the bouncy, fun piece of music. One part sounded as if a row of cancan dancers were about to leap onto the ice with her.

Tori began with lively opening steps, followed by a double axel. She held the landing until she was sure every judge had seen.

Tori realized that she hadn't been smiling when she landed the jump. Concentrate! she told herself. She pumped her legs in powerful back crossovers, with a few turns and an arabesque, until she was at the other end of the rink. Now it was time for a tough combination jump: a triple Lutz–double toe loop. Tori nailed the combination. Yes! she thought. She sailed through the Mohawk turns that brought her around the rink again.

She was breathing heavily by this time. It's too early to be tired, she thought. What if I've used up all my energy?

She tried to control her breathing. She tightened her body and threw herself into a layback spin. She came out of the spin and did two back crossovers. Then she stretched her leg back for an intricate spiral sequence.

Next came her spin combination. Spins didn't get the audience as excited as spectacular jumps did, but they were difficult. Especially when you're tired, she thought. Tired and maybe really sick.

Suddenly Tori pictured Dr. Mitchell, with his goatee and young face. She could hear him telling her that she had myotonic muscular dystrophy.

MD.

I have MD.

I shouldn't even be out here! she thought.

She wobbled as she lowered herself into a sit spin. Then she did a back sit spin. With a flourish, she stood and grabbed her left foot, pulling it high over her head.

The crowd applauded enthusiastically. Didn't they see how sloppy my sit spin was? Tori thought. I can't mess up like that again!

She stroked down the ice, breathing heavily but forcing herself to smile. At the other end of the rink she got ready for her triple loop. She hurled herself into the jump.

It was wrong from the start. She could feel it. She didn't have enough height in her jump. In a split second, she had to decide whether to turn the triple into a double . . . or hit the ice with a thud on her behind.

She did both.

She heard the crowd gasp as she fell. The jarring thud jangled her teeth together. She blinked hard against the pain and popped right up. She smiled and moved smoothly back into her routine.

But she wanted to cry. She wanted to skate off the ice. She wanted her mother to hug her and tell her everything would be all right.

She did a straight-line step sequence, including bracket hops, chocktaws, and twizzles. She forced herself to keep smiling as she hopped along with can-canlike kicks.

The last fifteen seconds went by in slow motion. She knew she had to end on a high note. She finished with a flying camel, which she hit perfectly.

The crowd clapped loudly. Tori bowed and waved. She skated toward the boards.

She had nailed most of her moves, except for the awful triple loop and the sloppy sit spin. But she had been concentrating so hard, she had forgotten to feel the music. And she hadn't made a connection with the audience and the judges. Her usual sparkle had been missing.

Tori stopped at the opening in the boards and stepped off the ice. Dan smiled encouragingly. She grabbed his hand and her mother's. The three of them walked to the area called the kiss-and-cry, where skaters waited for their scores.

Tori and Dan sat on the small bench as Mrs. Carsen stood nearby. Tori watched the electronic scoreboard anxiously. She was still breathing hard, and her legs were starting to cramp up.

The numbers finally flashed across the board. Tori was in third place. She knew she should be glad. It was a good score, considering the competition she was up against. But Amber still hadn't skated. If Amber got a higher score, Tori would be knocked into fourth place.

She tried to smile. She was painfully aware of the looming television cameras pointing at her face. Dan squeezed her hand.

"That's a very good score," he said quietly. "Don't worry about not placing first. You're still in the running."

The applause faded and the next skater began. Dan put an arm around Tori and looked into her eyes.

"Are you sure you're feeling all right?" he asked.

"Didn't you just tell me my scores were good?" Tori asked.

"The scores were fine. Your skating was fine. But I saw you breathing hard, sweating. You looked exhausted out there. And you were concentrating so hard on your program, you forgot you were performing for an audience, too."

"I know that already, Dan," Tori snapped.

He sighed. "Look, I don't want to bug you. But since you fainted in Seneca Hills, I've been worried."

Tori didn't know what to say. She hadn't realized Dan was worried about her. But she couldn't tell him the truth now.

"Dan, I went to the doctor this morning. He gave me a clean bill of health. He says I'm fine!" She grinned at him, feeling bad about the whopping lie.

She looked up and saw that her mother was standing just behind Dan. Mrs. Carsen's forehead wrinkled and she shook her head slowly. Tori shot her mother a warning look.

Mrs. Carsen forced herself to smile as she walked up to Tori and hugged her tightly.

"That's right," she told Dan. "Tori's doing fine."

Dan nodded, but he didn't look convinced.

"I've got to go prepare Amber for her program," he said. "I'll call you tonight at the hotel, Tori."

Mrs. Carsen turned back to Tori. Her smile faded away.

"Come with me," she said. She hurried Tori to a private corner in the locker room.

"Sit down," she commanded. "Let me feel your muscles." She ran her hands down Tori's legs, massaging them. "You're as hard as a rock. You're stiff, tight, and exhausted." She sighed. "Whatever you have, it's really robbing you of your strength."

Tori twirled her ankle slowly and winced. Her muscles felt like iron. But her mother's words rang in her ears.

"Whatever you have," she had said. Her mom knew that *something* was wrong. But she didn't believe Tori had muscular dystrophy.

Tori's right calf seized up in a painful spasm. She reached down to massage it herself. As she did, she realized something frightening.

Maybe mom's right, and I don't have MD. But there's something very wrong with me. And if it gets any worse, I'm not just going to mess up my long program on Saturday. I'm not even going to finish it!

America's Top Singles Skaters

Michelle Kwan

Michelle Harvath

At seventeen, Michelle Kwan is hoping to bring home a gold medal from the 1998 Olympics.

She won gold at the 1996 U.S. Championships. She was only fifteen at the time, which made her the youngest national champion since Peggy Fleming in 1964. (Tara Lipinski has since beaten this record.) Again in 1996, Michelle won gold at the World Championships, becoming one of the youngest champions ever.

1

Michelle doesn't think being young is a disadvantage. She says her victories are "a matter of hard work and discipline and having a clear focus on your goals. That can happen at any age."

Michelle comes from a skating family. Her older sister, Karen, is also a senior-level skater who's had lots of success. Michelle began skating at age five, after watching her big brother Ron play ice hockey. She won her first competition at age seven.

Michelle is allowed chocolate only once a week. But since she loves treats, she's created a special health drink. She tosses sugar-free cocoa, nonfat milk, ice cubes, and a banana into a blender. After a quick stir, she's got a nutritious shake.

Michelle's combination of artistry and athleticism makes her a strong competitor. On the ice she's coolly elegant as she lands triple jump after triple jump. Still, she knows that a skater can always use something extra, so she wears a Chinese good-luck charm around her neck. It was a gift from her grandmother.

Stats:

Michelle was born July 7, 1980, in Torrance, California. She is five feet, two inches tall and weighs 100 pounds. Training town: Lake Arrowhead, California.

Tara Lipinski

Paul Harvath

Short *but good.*

That's what it says on the necklace Tara Lipinski wears. It's true. Tara *is* short. In 1997, at age fifteen, she stood only four feet, eight inches tall. But Tara is also very good.

This petite skater has been called a jumping machine. During the 1997 U.S. Championships, she landed *seven* triple jumps—and won. That same year, she won the World Championships. At fourteen, she became the youngest female skater ever to win the world figure-skating title.

Tara began roller skating at age three. She switched to figure skating at six. Even then, she set her sights high. She likes to tell the story of how she asked her dad to build three boxes. She lined them up to be her pretend victory podium. She would stand on the top box and imagine the gold medal being draped around her neck.

Her dream might come true at the 1998 Winter Olympics. Tara is considered a top contender for the gold medal. And if it doesn't happen in 1998, there are always the Olympics in 2002—or even 2006.

Stats:

Tara was born June 10, 1982, in Philadelphia.
She is four feet, eight inches tall and weighs seventy-five pounds.
Training town: Bloomfield Hills, Michigan.

Nicole Bobek

Michelle Harvath

Some call it star quality or crowd appeal. Some call it sparkle. Whatever you call it, Nicole Bobek has it.

Audiences go wild for this striking twenty-year-old skater. They love to watch her trademark spiral spin, in which she extends her leg gracefully behind her and stretches it high over her head.

In the past, Nicole's coaches had trouble taming her

wild spirit. Her happy-go-lucky ways interfered with the discipline she needed to become a champion.

Lately, though, all that has changed. Nicole is working harder than ever. She has earned the respect of fans, fellow skaters, and judges with her new polish on the ice. She won the 1995 U.S. Nationals and finished third in 1997. Could she turn out to be the star of the 1998 Winter Olympics? At the moment, it's a definite possibility.

Stats:

Nicole was born August 23, 1977, in Chicago.
She is five feet, five inches tall and weighs 120 pounds.
Training town: Lake Arrowhead, California.

Todd Eldredge

Michelle Harvath

Todd Eldredge is one of skating's hardest workers. He once traveled to a skating event in Canada, but not to skate. He wanted to check out the competition!

Todd is a fisherman's son from Chatham, Massachusetts. He received his first pair of hockey skates at age five. Within two weeks, he switched to figure skates. Since then, he's won titles at all three skating levels—

novice, junior, and senior. He's a four-time U.S. champion.

Todd has had his share of disappointments, too. He placed only tenth in the 1992 Winter Olympics. At times, he has even considered quitting skating. But never for very long. His love of the sport keeps him coming back to the ice.

Todd is known for the long hours of practice he puts in, and his determination has paid off. He was the 1996 world champion. In one year—1997—he won the gold at the Nationals and the silver at the World Championships.

But another challenge lies ahead. "I've won the Nationals, and won the Worlds. I don't have that Olympic medal," he says. "That's definitely high on my list of priorities."

Stats:

Todd was born August 28, 1971, in Chatham, Massachusetts.

He is five feet, eight inches tall and weighs 145 pounds.

Training town: Bloomfield Hills, Michigan.

Dan Hollander

Paul Harvath

There's a whole lot of energy packed into this five-foot-two-inch, 126-pound skater. He competes using everything he's got.

Dan blends showmanship with technical skill to come up with a winning combination. And he has the medals to prove it. He won the bronze medal at the U.S. Championships in 1996 and 1997. He wears a ring that says it all: *phil sung*. That's Korean for "certain victory."

Dan began skating at the age of four, when he tagged along to the ice rink with his sister Sandra. He wanted to play ice hockey. But after he saw a photo of a bashed-up hockey player, he decided figure skating might be less dangerous.

Off the ice, Dan never rests. He holds a red belt in Choi Kwang Do. He also enjoys in-line skating, skateboarding, and playing racquetball.

Stats:

Dan was born May 9, 1972, in Royal Oak, Michigan.
He is five feet, two inches tall and weighs 126 pounds.
Training town: St. Clair Shores, Michigan.

Michael Weiss

Michelle Harvath

Michael Weiss, an outstanding athlete, comes from a family of outstanding athletes. Greg and Margie Weiss, his parents, are gymnasts who made the 1960 and 1964 Olympic gymnastics team. Michael's older sister Genna won a junior World diving title. His other older sister, Geremi, finished second in the junior division of women's figure skating at the Nationals.

Like Genna, Michael is a terrific diver. He's a former

regional diving champion. He first became interested in skating at age nine, when he tagged along with Geremi to the practice rink.

Michael is a well-rounded athlete. His hobbies include volleyball, tennis, golf, in-line skating, hockey, and weight training. His energy and hard work don't end with sports—he somehow finds time to study hard, too. He recently graduated with honors from Prince Georges Community College in Maryland.

In 1997 Michael won the silver medal at the U.S. Championships. The highlight of his performance was his powerful quadruple toe jump. The 1998 Olympic Games will be Michael's most exciting challenge yet.

Stats:

Michael was born August 2, 1976, in Washington, D.C.
He is five feet, eight inches tall and weighs 160 pounds.
Training town: Fairfax, Virginia.

DO YOU HAVE A YOUNGER BROTHER OR SISTER?

Maybe he or she would like to meet Jill Wong's little sister Randi and her friends in the exciting new series

SILVER BLADES®

FIGURE EIGHTS

Look for these titles at your bookstore or library:

ICE DREAMS
STAR FOR A DAY
THE BEST ICE SHOW EVER!
BOSSY ANNA
DOUBLE BIRTHDAY TROUBLE
SPECIAL DELIVERY MESS
RANDI'S MISSING SKATES
MY WORST FRIEND, WOODY
RANDI'S PET SURPRISE
And coming soon:
RANDI GOES FOR THE GOLD!